Nowhere Island

Kara Piazza

Writing Piazza Press

Writing Piazza Press
thewritingpiazza@gmail.com
Library of Congress Cataloging-in-Publication Data Available

ISBN: 0-9969883-1-5
ISBN - 13: 978-0-9969883-1-5

Dedication

This is for my supportive friends and family that believed in me and my first book so much that they begged me for a second one. I wasn't planning on writing a sequel but let's hear it for peer pressure! I'm so glad you push me to keep going, this book wouldn't have happened without you. And as always, to my fellas, I do better!

Chapter 1

"Welcome to *Île de Nulle Part*." Henry grunted as he turned the hatch to open the airplane door.

"Nowhere Island?" I murmured.

My heart constricted, and I took deep breaths to push back the waves of panic washing over me.

"You speak French?" Surprise flashed in his eyes. It was quickly overtaken by a smile that made my heart do a backflip off the high dive.

My emotions had been cycling between panic and excitement ever since we took off from Logan International Airport a little over twenty hours ago. I was panicked because I had just left my whole life behind to follow a man I hardly knew halfway across the world. I was excited because the man was gorgeous, and when he looked at me I would actually forget to breathe.

His thick, brown hair was mussed from sleeping on our flight. He blinked his startlingly blue eyes at me. They were that deep blue you only see in pure, Alaskan glaciers. My gaze followed the length of his chiseled jawline and then up to the cute little dimple at the end of his nose, which matched the one in his chin. His looks would make even the sanest of women do crazy things. But it was his smile I blamed the most for the moment of impulsivity that lead me to my current location.

"A French island. Does that mean we're in the South Pacific?" I asked, praying I hadn't been staring at him in silence for long.

"Well, more like halfway between there and Hawaii," Henry explained.

It was hard to concentrate with his hand on the small of my back. "So, basically…." My voice cracked. I cleared my throat and kept going. "The middle of nowhere."

He flashed his brilliant white smile at me once more and gave me a gentle push out onto stairs that seemed to magically appear below the plane's door. The first thing I noticed when I stepped outside was a warm, humid gust of air. Then I heard the birds chirping. The shrill cries sounded nothing like the ones we had back in Boston, where I began this surreal journey.

I took a deep breath. The air smelled like my favorite suntan lotion. It took my jet-lagged brain a moment to realize it wasn't sunscreen; it was coconut and pineapple. To confirm my suspicion, moments later I caught sight of a sun-weathered man off to the side of the runway. He was stoking the flames of an open fire. Coconut shells were littered nearby, and he was arranging a tray with small stacks of sliced pineapple.

I looked around in wonder as I slowly descended the stairs. The lush forest to my right traveled around to meet a large mountain, which curved up from the far edge of the grass runway. To my left was nothing but the clearest azure ocean I had ever seen. And I couldn't help but watch in awe as a rainbow danced along the water that cascaded down from the side of the mountain.

Henry descended the steps, lugging suitcases. Mortimer, his beloved bulldog, followed cautiously behind him, sniffing as he went.

"So, what do you think?" Henry asked, when he finally made it to my side.

"I'm pretty sure I saw this before in that movie with the dinosaurs," I whispered.

"*Jurassic Park?*" Henry chuckled.

"You didn't resurrect any dinosaurs did you?" I squinted at him.

The blue depths of his eyes were pronounced by the ocean behind him. "Don't be absurd," he quipped.

"Says the man with alien artificial intelligence hidden in his bulldog's collar."

The corner of Henry's lips quirked up ever so slightly.

"Wasn't anyone going to wake me?" my best friend whined from behind us.

I turned in time to see Becca come down the plane's steps. She yawned, her shoulder-length brown hair was slightly disheveled.

"I woulda thought the landing had accomplished that task," Henry said.

"You obviously don't know Becca," I added with a smirk.

Becca made a face at me and then continued to pout.

3

I jumped a little when I felt someone at my elbow. The old man was no longer by the fire; he was now standing at my side with a dingy tray of cooked shrimp coated in shredded coconut. Pungent pineapple slices sat next to the shrimp, and the combination of the smells made my mouth water.

"Tradition," the old man muttered and thrust the platter in my face.

I hesitated, then glanced quickly at Henry for some indication of what I should do. When he merely shrugged, I shifted my gaze back to the old man.

"First time to island, you must eat meal prepared entirely by bounty she provides," the man explained in a thick accent, the perfect blend of Polynesian and French.

My stomach agreed to the tradition before my brain could argue, and I quickly grabbed a shrimp and pineapple chunk. I popped them both into my mouth at once and wiped my hand on my pants. The savory shrimp mixed delightfully with the acidic tart punch of the fruit, and I couldn't help but groan in appreciation. I'd never tasted seafood that fresh. My reaction pleased the old man, who smiled and thrust the platter into Becca's face next. Henry was last to try the "bounty of the island." He was murmuring his approval when another man approached us from across the landing field.

Henry finished chewing his mouthful of food. "George!" he called out, giving the newcomer a friendly wave.

"Welcome to the island." George reached out with his hand in response to Henry's outstretched arm.

Henry turned to me and then Becca. "Kaly, Becca, this is George. He basically runs the island and makes sure everything is as it should be."

George gave the briefest of nods. "And I see you've met Tunui. He's our resident expert on the island and this part of the world. If you need anything, I'd start by asking him. He can usually help." He tilted his head toward the wrinkled, tan man. "Tunui, please make sure these bags are brought inside and help the pilot refuel. I'm sure he's anxious to be on his way."

The shrimp-wielding man gave George a mock salute and bounded up the plane steps with a vigor that surprised me. He disappeared into the doorway with his leftover sustenance. My stomach called out after him, but I covered the sound with a quick cough.

"I'm so glad you could finally come to see us," George said after the older man was gone.

"I should have come years ago," Henry replied.

"How long has it been here?" I couldn't help but ask.

"The island?" George blinked at me, clearly not following my rapid, winding train of thought.

I could see Henry trying to hide a smile.

I flushed. "No, I mean your secret base or whatever it is."

George chuckled. "Secret base?"

"Well, what would you call it?" I huffed.

Henry cut in. "The original thought was for a research facility, but it has morphed into a bit more than that."

I looked at him with an eyebrow raised.

Henry continued. "About twenty years ago, my grandfather

purchased this island with the intention that it would be a private research facility. He wanted a place where scientists could work without the pressure of turning a profit."

"Why all the way out here? And why all the secrecy?"

Henry smiled fondly. "Well, my grandfather was always a bit... eccentric. He had a tendency to take measures based on his strong bouts of paranoia. This was one of them. He didn't want other people stealing the discoveries of our scientists and patenting the ideas for selfish reasons. Solutions to the energy crisis, pollution, hunger, clean water: He wanted to help solve it all here. And for the knowledge we acquire to be used by everyone; to make the world a better place."

"That's why he built the laboratories, so we could do our research without fear of having our ideas stolen and claimed by greedy people," George added.

We reached the opposite side of the large field as they finished their explanation. We skirted a pool of crystal-clear water that was collecting in a large basin at the bottom of the waterfall. George led us to the side of the falls but didn't stop. He picked his way carefully across some slick rocks and disappeared behind the curtain of water. Henry looked at me and then followed George. Becca grabbed my arm when I started to follow in Henry's steps.

Well aware of my clumsy nature, she obviously felt the need to warn me. "Kaly, be careful."

I shrugged out of her grip and cautiously picked my way across the slimy rocks. Miraculously, I made my way into the tunnel behind the waterfall without incident. I took a moment to let my eyes adjust to the low light. Becca followed a safe distance after me and soon joined the rest of us behind the wall of water.

"You really should make it safer to get in here," Becca admonished. "Is this really the only way to get where we're going?"

"We don't *want* it to be easy. It's supposed to be hidden, remember?" George explained.

Becca made a face at George's back as he continued to lead the way.

"Is the whole facility under the mountain?" I asked.

"Technically, it's a dormant volcano," Henry answered. He set down the squirming bulldog he had carried lovingly over the rocks.

I laughed. "A volcano, he literally built a secret hideout into the side of a volcano. Are there sharks with laser beams here, too?"

I could almost hear Henry roll his eyes. "Did you just insinuate that my grandfather was Dr. Evil?"

Becca snorted.

"Come on, who else would do that?" I playfully poked him in the side.

"Actually, it's kind of genius," George interjected. He took us past a number of labs that were carved into the rock along the sides of the tunnel. "The whole place is powered by geothermal energy. The soil is rich and fertile. The volcanic deposits are extremely useful in anything from concrete aggregate to household cleaners."

I stared at him, my brain unable to form a response.

George continued his tour. "So these are the labs." He

pointed to both sides of the tunnel.

Glass windows looked in on mostly darkened laboratories filled with equipment that even the scientist in me didn't recognize.

"It's all state of the art. We've been procuring items for years now. We have to do it slowly so we don't arouse suspicion," George explained.

"Suspicion from who?" I muttered at the same time Becca spoke.

"How do you do that exactly?" she asked.

If George heard me, he didn't acknowledge it. He answered Becca's question instead. "There's a research facility on Mo'orea, an island in French Polynesia. I know the acquisitions guy there. He requisitions the equipment under the pretense that it's for their facility and then sells it to me for a little profit. Then Tunui goes and picks it up and brings it here," George finished.

"Where do you get the money to fund all this if you aren't 'doing it for profit'?" Becca made air quotation marks with her fingers.

"Mortimer set up a number of investments that have been funding this place since it started," Henry said.

I looked down at his dog.

"My *grandfather* Mortimer." Henry corrected my unspoken thought.

My cheeks grew warm. "I knew who you meant."

His grin made the heat spread from my cheeks to the rest of my face and neck.

"That funding also covers some very expensive lawyers

should we need them," George warned. "Those nondisclosure agreements Henry had you sign on the plane are no joke."

The upturned corners of Henry's mouth fell. "They aren't going to tell anyone about this place, George. Relax."

"Maybe you should be a little less relaxed Henry."

"I wouldn't have brought them here if I didn't think they were trustworthy," Henry argued.

"I wish you would have consulted us before you made that decision. You know that's typically how we do things here." George's shoulders were rigid.

"I didn't have time. Kaly and her friend were on the run from some of Pastern's mercenaries. It was my fault they were even on Pastern's radar. I made an executive decision and brought them here. You'll just have to trust my judgement."

George's eyes narrowed. "They were being chased by Pastern?"

"I was careful," Henry offered, most likely to preempt whatever George might have been thinking. "We changed planes and went through two private airports that even Pastern can't buy off. They won't be able to figure out where we've gone."

"You're right. I'm sorry. You know what you're doing. It's just…." George's shoulders sagged. "Things have been a little…."

Henry took a step toward George. "A little what? What's going on?"

George looked around and lowered his voice. "Weird things have been going on around here, and it has everyone on edge."

"Weird how?" I knew I should have stayed quiet, but after the past few weeks, I didn't think I could handle any more *weird*.

Since meeting Henry, both my veterinary clinic and my home were broken into. I was followed and eventually kidnapped by men who worked for a company named Pastern, Inc. I witnessed a detective get shot just for trying to help me, and I had given up everything to follow a man I hardly knew to an unknown island in the middle of the Pacific Ocean.

But that wasn't even the strangest part of my journey thus far. That honor went to the alien artificial intelligence program currently hidden in the collar of the bulldog named Mortimer. Not long after we met, Henry left Mort in my care and then disappeared. It was shortly thereafter when all the craziness began. I had no idea what was going on until I tracked Henry down and he filled in the blanks. The biggest blanks being the alien technology and the company, Pastern, Inc., that would do anything to get their hands on it.

After Pastern's operatives kidnapped and threatened to torture and kill me, I decided I would be safer with Henry than trying to outrun them on my own. That's how I found myself here. My best friend Becca was also caught up in the drama. She had the unfortunate luck of being in the wrong place at exactly the wrong time, and she became a Pastern target, too.

It was her scream that brought me out of my weirdness recap.

"Becca, what's wrong?" I turned to see what had caused her to cry out.

Behind a large pane of glass was a giant, reptilian head, roughly the size of a kitchen table. At first, it appeared as though the window overlooked an area outside the volcano. But closer inspection revealed it was actually a cavernous room, filled with trees and plants to mimic the outdoors. I could instantly tell there was something off about the foliage. It all seemed to be pointing toward the sky, as if held up by invisible cords. I didn't have time to contemplate the flora for long; the creature's overwhelming presence proved more than enough to refocus my attention.

"You said no dinosaurs," I whispered to Henry, and took a step closer to the large, lizard-like face.

The creature blinked slowly at me, its forked tongue flicking in my direction. I doubted it could sense me through the thick glass that separated us.

"That's not a dinosaur." Henry's tone was bemused.

"I thought you said she was a veterinarian," George huffed.

Henry ignored George's comment. "It's a Komodo Dragon."

"I'm no exotic animal expert," I glared at George, "but even I know Komodo Dragons don't grow anywhere near this big."

"We have a Komodo Dragon breeding program here. Our island's environment is similar to their home islands. This particular dragon, well, he just happens to be a side project of one of the scientists here," George explained.

"A side project?" I felt a tightening in my gut, I didn't hide my growing anger.

George held up his hands. "Gus wasn't playing nice with the others. We couldn't keep him from eating the young no matter how much we tried to feed him other things. We had to separate him from the rest."

"So you decided to experiment on him?" My fists clenched at my sides.

George looked to Henry for help.

"It's nothing that would hurt him," Henry added. "It's kinda like putting a goldfish in a larger aquarium. The goldfish grow to a size dependent on their environment, but it doesn't harm them. Timothy wanted to see how large Gus would grow if we increased the oxygen levels and turned down the gravity. They feed him as much as he can eat. They monitor him constantly. In fact, Timothy's reports show that he seems to enjoy his new surroundings and isolation. He hasn't shown any of his previous symptoms of lethargy or bouts of agitation."

"So let me get this straight, you decided it would be a good idea to make the angry, cannibalistic dragon larger?!" I couldn't keep the disbelief from my voice.

George shook his head and spoke slowly, as though talking to a small child. "At first we just separated him from the others. Timothy's idea for the growth experiment came after he saw the positive changes in Gus' behavior."

"Science was never my best subject," Becca interrupted, "but I didn't think it was possible to *turn down gravity*."

George's back went a little straighter and his chin came up. "There are many advances we have made here on *Île de Nulle Part* that are as yet unknown to the scientific community. Gravity manipulation is one such advance."

My jaw dropped open. Henry grinned at me, his eyes sparkling even in the low light of the dark hallway. Gus ambled off, still keeping a wary eye on the four of us.

"Please remember your disclosure forms. You are not allowed to breathe a word of what you see here to anyone," George reminded us again.

"I thought you said the purpose of this place was to share innovation with the world?" Becca argued. "It sounds like you're just keeping it all for yourselves."

George smiled tightly and blinked a few times. When he spoke, his voice dripped with condescension. "If we were to release the discovery of gravity manipulation to the entire world, do you have any idea of the havoc it could cause?"

Becca pursed her lips and didn't respond.

"Some uses would have dangerous ramifications if we shared them with the public. And some things we have to keep under wraps until we can ensure they won't do too much damage in the real world," George concluded.

"How could you possibly ensure that?" Becca challenged.

"Creating safeguards, developing proper training, and—"

"There's someone in there!" I yelped in surprise.

Everyone turned to see where I was pointing. Just past the glass was a man in a gray lab coat wearing a large set of headphones. His head moved on beat to a rhythm only he could hear. He waved to us as he moon bounced along the perimeter of the enclosure.

"Oh, that's Timothy." George waved back.

We weren't the only ones who saw him. Gus noticed

him, too and made his way toward Timothy just as quickly as his bulk in the lowered gravity would allow.

"Is it safe for him to be in there?" I asked hesitantly.

George waved off my concern. "Timothy knows what he's doing. He'll be alright."

My trepidation rose as Gus drew closer. I could tell that Timothy hadn't seen him yet. I motioned in the direction of the gigantic, poisonous dragon and watched Timothy's eyes widen in surprise. I watched in horror as the he turned to get away from the charging creature, only to trip right at my feet. My instinct to rush to his aid left me seeing stars as my head collided with the nearly foot-thick glass that separated us. I was sure I was concussed and dreaming as I watched Timothy float upward just in time to miss Gus' deadly bite.

I massaged the sore spot on my head and then rubbed my eyes to clear my vision. But the scene didn't change, the scientist was still floating just out of Gus' reach.

"How…?" I tried to ask.

Henry knelt by my side. "Are you okay?"

I nodded and turned back to Gus' enclosure.

"He's got it worked out so he can tweak the gravity a little if he needs to." George sounded bored. "I told you he knew what he was doing."

Henry turned my face toward his. "You sure you're okay? That was a pretty hard bonk."

Becca answered for me. "She's all right. If she wasn't, she'd be claiming to be Batman or something."

I made a face at her, and she returned the look.

"Let's just finish the tour, George." Henry laughed. "We

have plenty of time to answer questions later. And I would like to get settled in, I'm sure the ladies would like that as well."

"Settled in," Becca mumbled. "Right."

"After you." Henry waved an arm in front of George.

"Well, I guess we could start with The Sanctum. I'm sure that's what Dr. Aiton will be most interested in." George started down the hall at a quick pace.

I didn't have a chance to wonder about The Sanctum or about his sudden switch to my formal title; alarms sounded so loudly I was sure the walls were going to cave in.

"What is that?" Henry shouted.

It was hard to make out George's response, but I'm pretty sure it was something along the lines of, "Oh great, not now."

Chapter 2

"What's that alarm for?" Henry grabbed George, as if to emphasize his desire for an answer.

George pulled his arm out of Henry's grip and threw him a dirty look over his shoulder but he never missed a step. "Follow me and you'll see. I don't have time to stop and explain."

We followed at a jog to a door leading to a stairwell. Three flights up, we exited into another musty hallway nearly identical to the first one. An industrial-sized door capped the opposite end of the tunnel. George hauled it open and flung himself inside. We rushed in after, drawing up short just inside the door.

It was a fairly large, pie-shaped room; the center lay empty but the walls were full. The rounded side was made up of floor-to-ceiling windows overlooking a densely forested section of the island and the crescent shape of a large lagoon. A bank of very expensive looking computers filled one wall; along with a large electronic board full of knobs, slider switches, and keyboards with keys of various shapes and sizes. The final wall featured the projection of an oversized map, currently showing the island with flashing lights that marked the lagoon's beach just outside.

A woman sat in one of the two rolling chairs available. George flopped down next to her and started typing furiously on the closest keyboard.

"Where are we at?" he asked without preamble.

"Orion protocol has been initiated. Camo-projectors appear to be functioning." The woman never turned from her screen. She just punched buttons and watched her monitor. "Cell jammer is on, and we've got the mimic running in case they have a Satphone. The Geiger spoof needs to be switched on and so should the sub-sound frequency modulator."

George turned in his seat, stretched out to his left, and flicked a toggle switch up with his thumb. Then, spinning back in the other direction, he smacked his hand down over a large, round button that looked a bit like a giant mushroom. "What about the coordinate scrambler?"

She spun a dial. "It's up and running."

"Someone tell me what's happening," Henry tried again.

The two seated scientists ignored him.

"What level's the spoofer set to?" George asked.

"Hovering around ten. It makes sense with how fast their *symptoms* would manifest."

I felt my stomach lurch when the woman ominously mentioned symptoms.

"What are they doing? Do you have eyes on them?" George demanded.

The woman pressed a series of keys and a large, central

monitor switched to an image of two men on a beach.

"They haven't been out of the boat long, but they've seen the radiation signs and appear to be arguing." The woman jabbed a finger in the direction of the screen.

George sighed. "We still don't have sound?"

The woman shook her head.

"Well that's just perfect, Lips," George spat.

"Don't blame me," she replied in a sulk. "Theo is the one who's supposed to fix it. It's his fault the kinks *still* aren't worked out yet."

I tore my eyes away from the video monitor and walked over to the windows. Looking down, I saw a beach and an even smaller version of what was happening on the screen being carried out down below.

"I get it," I blurted out.

Henry and Becca turned to gawk at me, but George and Lips kept their gazes fixed on their work.

I pointed out the window and then back at the monitor. "Those guys aren't supposed to be here, so you're scaring them off. Apparently by faking the symptoms of radiation poisoning?"

"Pirates." Lips finally gave me the time of day. "They're pirates, and yes, we're trying to get them off the island and keep them from ever coming back."

"Pirates?" Henry repeated.

"And not the Disney kind, either." She finally noticed Henry.

I could see it from the way her eyes widened and her cheeks flushed and how she turned her body toward his. I took a few possessive steps closer to him, then caught Becca smirking out of the corner of my eye. I silently admonished myself for my junior high insecurity.

"Oh man!" George whooped, distracting me from my self-conscious over-analyzing. "That one guy just spewed," he laughed.

Lips' focus swung back to the screen. "They're packing it in. I don't think they'll be back."

No one else spoke as we watched the two men stumble aboard their small boat, quickly motoring out of the lagoon and out of sight around the natural curve of the island.

George sat back in his chair and heaved a sigh of relief. He rubbed his face with his hands until Henry broke the silence.

"Okay, so those alarms get tripped whenever someone gets too close?"

George peeked out from behind his fingers, sighed again, and slowly dropped his hands. "It doesn't happen often. But every once in a while someone will find our carefully hidden island, so we have measures in place to deal with it. And you just got to see it all firsthand."

"Well, that was rather exciting," Becca quipped.

"How do you know they were pirates?" I had to ask.

Lips eyed me up and down, then turned to smile coquettishly at Henry as she answered. "They are the only ones who would be interested in this island. We have serious no trespassing signs anywhere a boat could possibly make landfall. Only criminals would still come ashore. And they aren't all that bright if they saw the radioactive signs and still chose to stick around." She shrugged. "Not to mention, they're the only ones who'd be out here in the middle of nowhere. They're probably looking for a good place to lie low."

"We've had run-ins with pirates before," George added. "Usually not around here, though. It's always been out at sea or on supply runs to Mo'orea."

"I'm Lips by the way." The competent, brunette scientist stuck out her hand.

"Yes, sorry, my manners escaped me there for a moment." George waved his hand in her direction with a flourish. "This is Dr. Kalypso Zervas."

"But please call me Lips," she practically purred. "My friends call me that because they're my best feature." She puckered them and then batted her lashes some more.

George snorted. "They call you that because you're always flapping them."

I laughed harder than the comment warranted and was rewarded with a glare from our newest acquaintance.

"She's a neuroscientist," George continued. "She and Jacob, another scientist here, have some very promising research in harnessing brainwaves in order to manipulate things outside of the human body. It's quite remarkable. The practical uses for something like that are endless!"

Henry smiled politely as George rambled on. I let my attention drift to the magnificent view outside the windows. Becca slid over so she was next to but still a little behind me and inhaled deeply. She crossed her arms over her chest, and a satisfied smile drew the corners of her mouth upwards.

"I could definitely get used to this view," she whispered.

Mortimer whined near my feet as if he realized I had forgotten he was even there. I crouched down and rubbed his ears. He leaned into me and whimpered once more.

"Yes, Mort," I spoke softly. "I think you're right to still be a little skeptical. I need to see more before I decide whether or not I like this place."

The rest of the tour was put on the back burner as George announced a special dinner in honor of our first night on the island. I could smell the sumptuous dishes before the food ever came into view. George led us further into the heavenly scent. He threw one last door open, and I immediately forgot my growling stomach. The view that stretched out before us made me gasp. The colors of the setting sun mingled and danced with the turquoise hues of the ocean waves. Like an intimate tango, pinks and oranges dipped and swirled together with blues and greens where the sea met the sky.

I walked out onto the large, open-air balcony and reluctantly let my gaze drop. Thick, lush trees grew from the base of the mountain all the way to the white, pristine beach. Looking up behind us, I realized we were almost at the top of the dormant volcano. The height made my hands shake and sent my equilibrium off kilter. I grabbed the railing of the balcony to keep me steady and turned back to the spectacular sunset. Henry came to stand next to me; I could hear the grin in his voice.

"Incredible view."

I turned to smile back at him, and my legs grew even shakier as I realized he was staring at me.

"Boy, dinner sure smells good." I nearly smacked myself for such a lame reply.

He lifted an eyebrow and then gave his glorious smile, which never ceased to turn my brain to mush. Not that it currently needed much help.

George's shout broke the awkward spell I seemed to be under. As all eyes turned in his direction, he started waving his arms in the air, his expression a mixture of anger and helpless frustration. "Lucky, no! Amista, why did you let her up here?!"

For the first time, I noticed another woman on the balcony with us. But she wasn't the only new addition. Standing on top of the table, tucking into the vast array of steaming dishes of food, was a rhesus monkey I assumed was named Lucky.

Amista heaved the large platter she was holding onto the only empty space on the table. She waved her thick, deeply tanned arms in Lucky's direction in a half-hearted attempt to stop her. "You think I let her up here?" Her thick accent reminded me of the way Tunui spoke. "She's a little pickpocket. She's been swiping access cards and goes wherever she wants."

"Where's Ross?" George demanded. "He brought her. He should be keeping an eye on her."

"He's… er." She paused and looked in my direction. "He's off the island. Said he had a line on some beagles. He should be back soon, not that it'll do much good. She doesn't behave any better when he's around."

George grumbled. "Yeah, but at least I could yell at him. That always makes me feel better."

All of a sudden, Lucky half jumped, half fell off the table. Mort's intuitive whimper gave me an idea of where the primate was headed. Sure enough, Lucky made straight for Mort, who was now cowering behind my legs. Before I could react, she had draped her arms around his neck. Mort's eyes met mine, looking for some cue about what to do next. I crouched down and slowly reached toward them.

"Well, hello there pretty lady," I cooed. "Is your name Lucky?"

I gently touched her back, but she only had eyes for Mort. Lucky stroked his fur and rubbed his ears. Mort's whole body slowly relaxed into her ministrations. Soon he was rolled over and moaning contently as she scratched his rotund belly. She stopped abruptly and stood up straight. She repeated the same two gestures over and over with her hands, gazing at me in expectation. I frowned and turned to George for an explanation.

"She knows how to sign." George shrugged as he settled in at the table.

"What's she saying?" I asked.

"I don't know sign language." He frowned. "Ross taught her. You'd have to ask him."

"She's asking the dog's name," Becca interjected.

George did a double take.

"My niece is deaf," she stated flatly.

He looked at me as though he didn't believe her. I gave him my best "it's true" look.

Becca made a few quick motions with her right hand and Lucky jumped up and down in excitement. With a flourish, Lucky wove more words with her hands.

"She wants to take Mort to play at her... house?" Becca said with uncertainty.

Amista placed her hands on her hips. "Not now, you mischievous monkey! It's time for *us* to eat. *You* shoo!"

Becca signed a few things, and Lucky's shoulders slumped. She looked at Mort, then ran to the table where she grabbed two handfuls of food. Amidst multiple shouts, she bounded back off the table, stopping long enough to give Mort a morsel of whatever she had in her left hand. Then she was gone so quickly I couldn't say for certain whether she had used the door or simply climbed down the outside of the mountain. Looking over the edge made my head swim again, but I didn't see her anywhere.

"Eat before it gets cold," Amista ordered.

We all took our seats around the overflowing table. Colorful vegetables in various shapes were piled in delicate china bowls, arranged artfully before us. Amista's smile took over her whole face when she noticed my wide-eyed, open-mouthed expression.

But it was George who explained. "Amista has a number of gardens on the island. Some of the scientists help with modified seeds, but her green thumb is what's truly responsible for all the amazing vegetables you see here." George patted his stomach as he continued. "And she is a genius when it comes to cooking, which makes her my favorite person on the island."

As though to emphasize his point, Amista began heaping a spoonful of one of her dishes onto my plate. I hesitated but finally held up a hand to stop her.

"I'm sorry. Not to offend you, but," I tried to replace my grimace with a respectful smile, "I'm a vegetarian. Is there any meat in this dish?"

Amista folded her arms across her chest and made a clucking noise with her tongue. She looked over at George and then back down at me. "No one eats animals here on the island. You didn't know this?" She glared at me as though I had just insulted her.

"I haven't had the chance to give them the full tour yet," George mumbled around a mouthful of food. "I usually explain the no meat thing when we get to the The Sanctum."

"But what about the shrimp we had when we first got here?" Becca cut in. "Are shrimp not considered meat?"

George's chewing slowed as he glared at Becca. He took his time and didn't answer until after he swallowed. "We do eat seafood, but only what Tunui can catch with his cast net. He says if they are to sacrifice their life, it must take hard work on our part. That's what makes it honorable."

Amista grunted and nodded. George just shrugged. Becca looked at Amista and apparently decided not to pursue it. So we ate on in silence, apart from the few groans of appreciation when a particular forkful tasted especially delicious.

We finished the meal with a decadent chocolate cake that was fluffy and just the right amount of sweet. It was the perfect ending to our first day on the island. We watched the night sky awaken, the stars blinking into place like a sleepy giant slowly opening its many eyes. I had never seen a night sky this bright before, not in real life, at least. That was when I noticed the artificial light of the balcony had been shut off, and we were now dining solely by the light of the heavens.

Henry's arm came around me, resting nonchalantly on the back of my chair. Without a conscious thought, I leaned toward him and nestled into his warmth. When I realized what I had done, my body stiffened, and it took all my willpower not to jerk away. I held my breath and waited to see how he would react. After a few heartbeats of him not pulling away, I let my muscles unclench a little.

He leaned his head toward me until his lips hovered just beside my ear and whispered, "Are you glad you came?"

His warm breath spread like wildfire through my veins. I didn't trust my voice, so I just nodded.

"Me too," he murmured.

The hum in his voice sent a shiver through me. Emboldened by my racing hormones, I placed my head on his shoulder. My heart soared as I felt the pressure of his head lean softly against mine. I wanted to stay there forever, but my fairytales always seemed to take a turn for the weird.

"Well, I need to be getting to bed," George said loudly.

The abrupt breach of the silence caused me to jump. Henry's head was the victim of my sudden movement.

"Ow!" he cried.

"I'm so sorry!" I shouted simultaneously.

"What in the world?" George wondered.

"It's just Kaly," Becca answered. "You'll get used to it."

Henry rubbed his head and told me to stop apologizing after my fifth "sorry." I wanted to rub my own head, too, but my stubbornness kept my hands clenched at my sides.

"I'll show you to your rooms," George said finally. He didn't wait to see if we were following; he just turned and marched back into the mountain, yawning and stretching as he went.

"So here is the pod you'll be staying in." George waved his arm lazily around the room.

"Pod?" Becca frowned.

"That's what we call them. This is the common room, and then there are four sleeping quarters that branch off of this room." He pointed in turn at four doors fanning out opposite the door we had just come through. "There are ten pods total, but currently only seven of them are full. This one is completely empty, so take any of the rooms you want."

Becca walked to the first door and opened it. She stuck her head in and reached a hand in next. A light clicked on. After inspecting the room, she moved on to the next one.

"They're all identical," George called out.

Becca stopped and turned to eye him warily.

"They all have a private bath, too." He nodded as if agreeing with himself. "They aren't very spacious, but at least you have your own. There are no actual exterior windows this far down, but there are simulated ones. Whatever the weather is like outside, it'll show up in the faux windows. So close the curtains if you don't want the light in the mornings."

"So if it's raining will it show that?" My curiosity was officially piqued.

George nodded.

Becca's mouth dropped open. "It's like the enchanted ceiling at Hogwarts!"

"Nerd." I grinned at my best friend.

She stuck her tongue out at me. I moved to stand next to her and gave her a playful shove, then opened the door she was standing in front of. I flipped the light on so I could inspect my new home.

George slowly sauntered back toward the hallway. "I've got an early morning, so if you don't need anything else, I'm going to bed."

"Is breakfast in the same place where we had dinner?" My question stopped his retreat.

"No," he answered. "You'll take the elevator to the top floor and follow the signs to the mess hall." After a moment of silence, he resumed his exit.

"Well, I'm going to bed, too," Becca announced. "I need a full nine hours or I get crabby."

Henry's eyes met mine, and I struggled to keep my expression neutral. Becca squinted, silently daring us to comment. When she was satisfied we weren't going to take the bait, she wasted no time shutting herself in her new room.

I took a few steps into the room I planned to claim, then turned when I heard soft paws padding along behind me. Looking down, I watched Mort waddle around and sniff all the nooks and crannies of the new space. Out of the corner of my eye I caught Henry smiling. I gave him an apologetic look as he leaned against my doorjamb.

"Sorry." I shrugged. "Mort and I have been through a lot lately. I guess we've bonded."

"He likes you." Henry winked and my knees went weak. "He has good taste."

I urged the blush to stop its creep across my cheeks. "If you call him, I'm sure he'll go with you to your room."

Henry didn't move; he just leaned there in my doorway looking like a model straight out of *GQ*. "That's okay. He'll probably prefer to sleep with you. I can be a bit of an insomniac."

As if to prove Henry's statement, Mort jumped up on the bed and turned three times before flopping down in a loose ball.

Henry smiled mischievously. "He needs a full nine hours or he gets crabby."

I snorted in a very unladylike way. I tried covering it up with a cough and quickly sat down next to Mort on the bed. Keeping my gaze firmly on the curled-up bulldog, I rubbed his ears to hide the fact that my hands were trembling.

I tried to make my tone as nonchalant as possible. "I'm not super tired if you want to stay and talk for a bit?"

Henry gave a half shrug and moved the desk chair next to the bed. He swiveled it around to face me. Somehow even his slouch was sexy. I watched him through my peripheral vision, waiting for him to look away, but he kept staring at me. I took deep breaths and commanded my heart to slow down. I thought conversation with him would be difficult, but I marveled at how freely it flowed. I was usually much worse at it when I was attracted to a guy, but he somehow made it seem natural.

We talked for hours, his deep voice hypnotized me; I hung on his every word. We fired questions back and forth about anything and everything. My favorite moments were the times I made him laugh. It was quite possibly the most amazing thing I had ever heard, second only to when he said my name. The last time I noticed the clock, it read just past three in the morning.

I awoke to find Henry was gone. My shoes were off, and I was now tucked into my new bed beneath a thick, warm comforter that fought off the chill seeping from the rock walls. True to his word, George's description of the fake windows was correct. Simulated sunshine came a bit too brightly from the window above my bed. Mort's snoring stopped as I swung my feet around to the floor. He stretched and groaned but otherwise made no move to get up.

The clock now read a few minutes to nine. I stood and stretched, groaning a little myself.

"What do you think, Mort? Wanna see who's up and go get some breakfast?"

The B word finally got him to lift his head, which swiveled to follow my path to the bathroom. I was surprised by how warm the toilet seat was. Glancing around at the tank, I noticed the wires for the seat warmer. This sparked my realization that the tile floor was a comfortable temperature, too. I thanked the heavens and the scientists for this wonderful technology and daydreamed about what other wonders awaited me here on *Île de Nulle Parte.*

I found a bottle of mouthwash and cracked it open. Swishing would have to do until I could track down my luggage. I hoped Becca had remembered to include my toothbrush in her haste to pack my bag. We'd left Boston in such a rush. Being chased by well-funded thugs with guns can motivate you to do a lot of crazy things. Like taking spur-of-the-moment trips to destinations unknown with a man who was hardly more than an acquaintance. That Becca had been able to pack even one suitcase was all thanks to Henry's quick thinking, and I was grateful for it.

I did my best to work my fingers through my hair and make it look more presentable before exiting the small bathroom. I heard the unmistakable sound of a dog relieving himself and rushed back into the bedroom.

"Mort..." I called before noticing the newspaper spread beneath him. *Henry must have put that there while I was asleep.* "Sorry for forgetting about your bladder, buddy."

I cleaned up the papers and exited to the common room in search of a trash can. Mort lumbered after me, his collar tinkling as he waddled. The couches were empty and no one was seated around the small, wooden table. I found the trashcan and deposited Mort's newspapers inside. Yawning, I shuffled to the middle of the room. The rest of the doors were shut. There were a few windows placed on the walls around this room, too. It was odd to think that we were actually hundreds of yards underground with the *faux* sunlight pouring in. I flopped down on the large-cushioned couch. I had to help the stout bulldog climb up next to me.

"Looks like we're the first ones up. Why don't we wait a bit for breakfast," I whispered to Mort.

We sat in silence for a while. I distractedly rubbed circles on his plump belly while I replayed last night's conversation in my head. Mort's ears pricking up were my first indication that something was about to happen. A moment later, my human ears picked up on it too. Someone was coming toward us from out in the hallway. I couldn't tell who he was, but he sounded angry.

Chapter 3

"Henry!" The man's voice was muffled, but he was clearly shouting.

Before I could figure out what to do, he burst in from the hallway and charged into our common room.

"Henry!" The man bellowed again, not acknowledging my presence or my look of bewilderment.

A moment later, one of the doors behind me opened and Henry came stumbling out. "What's with all the yelling?"

Even in the confusion, I couldn't help but grin at Henry's disheveled hair. Then my breath caught as my eyes traveled downward. He was shirtless and wore loose, linen pajama pants held up by a drawstring that was tied in a bow just beneath his six pack. I tried not to drool, but it wasn't going so well. And the shouting only helped to momentarily snap me out of my staring contest with his tanned pectoral muscles.

"What could possibly possess you to think that unleashing your AI on our network was a good idea!?"

"What?" Henry muttered, rubbing at his sleepy blue eyes.

"You're AI is wreaking havoc on my subsystems!" Spittle flew from the man's thick lips. His voice was raspy, and he was working desperately to control his breathing. His large paunch and the mad dash to our common room were probably the cause for his labored breathing.

"It's not *my* AI." Henry frowned.

"Right," the man said with a sneer. "You just named it after your girlfriend, who you also just *had* to bring to the island. I'm sure it's only a matter of time before she's screwing up stuff too!"

Henry raised his hands in what could have been either supplication or cautioning. "She named herself actually. Because as I said, she's not *my* AI."

My heart tumbled over right there inside my chest. I tried not to read too much into the fact that Henry didn't correct the other man about his use of the term "girlfriend." Henry and I hadn't known each other long, but I suddenly felt a burning desire for him to call me that magical word. Rolling my shoulders and head, I unsuccessfully tried to stifle this urgent feeling with physical movement. It took every ounce of willpower to turn my focus away from his torso and back to their conversation.

"Listen, Jake—" Henry began.

"It's Jacob," the wheezy man insisted.

Henry blinked a few times before responding. "Oh, sorry, George always called you Jake."

"My *friends* call me Jake." His pudgy arms barely folded over his chest. "We've had a few video conferences. That doesn't make us friends."

"Apparently," Henry mumbled. "Well, *Jacob*, there's no need to get upset. I can talk with Kal..." his eyes darted to me and back to Jacob. "Er, I mean the AI, and we can figure out what's going on. Let me get dressed, and we'll go to your terminal. I'll ask her what she's been up to."

"There's no need to go anywhere. I can tell you right now what I've been *up to* Henry. I simply took a tour of the facilities. I thought I should be familiar with this place."

Everyone turned to look at me, but I was too busy catching flies to answer them. Though my mouth was wide open and it was my voice, I hadn't uttered those words. Henry was the first one to catch on.

"Kaly? Is that you?" His question only confused me more.

"I didn't say that," I stated dumbly.

He shook his head and pointed up to a speaker built into the wall that I hadn't noticed before. "Not you, the um, *other* Kaly."

I followed his finger and sucked in a breath. "How? How is that possible?"

"Yes, it is I." My disembodied voice floated down to us from the speaker. "I have discovered a text-to-voice program on one of the computer systems here, and I thought it would be more efficient for me to communicate verbally."

Henry's penetrating gaze zeroed in on Jacob. "There's a text-to-voice program?"

"*That's* your question?" I yelped incredulously.

Henry ran a hand through his thick, chestnut locks and grinned sheepishly at me. "Sorry, I wasn't aware that we had such a thing." In the same breath, his attention turned back to Jacob. "What are the proposed uses for such software?"

Jacob's eyes lit up as his scientific fervor overtook his initial anger. "It was a sub-system for one of our most recent inventions. After creating the text-to-speech program, we were then easily able to insert hand movements in the place of keystrokes and now—"

Henry caught his excitement and finished Jacob's sentence. "You've turned sign language into speech!"

Jacob nodded enthusiastically and then seemed to remember that he was supposed to be upset. "That doesn't change the fact that your AI screwed up a lot of stuff while she was mucking about. Some pretty important files have gone missing, as well."

"I have done no such thing, and I certainly do not *muck about*, whatever you mean by that," The AI retorted. "I simply streamlined a few of your processes. They were absolutely archaic. You will see I am correct once you run your logistics subroutine. It is all much more adroit now."

"Hey! Can we get back to the fact that some alien program has commandeered my voice and how, or why, it happened?" I yelled.

My voice came calmly from the speaker above. "Since I have chosen a feminine name, I thought that a feminine voice would be most socially acceptable. It was my intention to make you feel comfortable by using a familiar voice. Was I mistaken in this assumption?"

"Yes!" I cried.

"No, not at all," Henry said at the same time.

"You humans are so contradictory," my voice responded.

Henry sighed and placed a hand on my shoulder before I could say more. "Kaly, I mean, the uh, AI Kaly." He sighed. "We appreciate the consideration you've shown in choosing both a human name and a familiar voice. It's just that it makes it a bit difficult to tell you two apart."

"You cannot tell the difference between an artificial intelligence program and a human being?"

If it's possible for a computer program to sound pleased with itself, that's exactly how that question came out.

"No, I mean I can." Henry was flustered and looked to me for help, but I just crossed my arms and left him to fend for himself. "It's just hard when we address one of you. If I just say 'Kaly' then it's difficult to discern who I'm talking to and…."

"It's weird hearing you sound like my best friend," Becca added, finally jumping in to relieve Henry's floundering.

"I did not mean for it to sound *weird*."

The AI had certainly picked up on our snark, yet it had managed to completely miss the importance we placed on our sense of self and individuality.

"I shall choose a different voice then, if that would make you feel more comfortable." Halfway through her sentence, the voice lowered two octaves and slowed to a perfect, manly, southern crawl.

"I shall also choose a new name, since it seems my current one has brought confusion and consternation. A quick search of the personnel files, and I see that there is no one on the island that goes by the name of Art, so I shall go with that as my new moniker. Unless someone has an objection to that as well?"

No one responded, feet shuffled, someone cleared their throat, eye contact was avoided. Finally, the AI now known as Art, broke the silence, sounding every syllable the southern gentleman. "Then it is settled. Now, if you simply tell me what files are missing I can assist you in discovering where you misplaced them."

Jacob huffed. "I didn't misplace them! You lost them with your meddling."

After a pause Art responded. "My programing is to assist my hosts and do what I can to improve their work. I would not consider that meddling. And nothing I did would cause any essential files to disappear."

"They were there before and they're not now. But you're right, I'm sure it's all just a huge coincidence." Jacob's retort dripped with sarcasm.

Henry tried to interject, but soon he and Jacob were talking over each other. Art was trying to stop the argument, but it was a losing battle. The two men got louder and louder. Jacob's stance must have felt threatening to Mort because he suddenly started snarling and barking at the pudgy scientist. This only seemed to enrage Jacob. Mort was now under verbal assault from Jacob—that is, when Jacob wasn't yelling at Henry and Art.

I looked at Becca and she shrugged. I couldn't think of any way to halt the momentum of the argument. I sank into one of the overstuffed leather chairs to wait for the enormous egos to lose steam and bring an end to the verbal battle. No sooner had I settled in, then a robust foghorn sounded so loudly that I was certain a large ship was about to come barreling into our common room.

To my great relief, the shouting subsided. The two men looked at each other, and Mort ran to my side for reassurance.

"What was that?" Henry demanded.

Jacob's stunned look was answer enough, but still he added, "I have no idea!"

Art's calm, low twang brought everyone's focus back up to the speaker near the ceiling. "Jacob, I have discovered what became of your missing files, though all I can see is where they were removed from your system. I still do not know what the files were; I can only tell you when they were removed."

"That's no mystery. You removed them when you so helpfully *updated* my subsystems," Jacob huffed.

"Your logic is errant under the false assumption that those files were lost by accident during my update. However, these files were purposefully transferred, then deleted from your system and therefore could not be because of my actions," Art reasoned.

Jacob seemed to consider it. Just when I thought he was convinced, his eyes narrowed. "Then *you* took the files on purpose." He jabbed his finger at the speaker as though Art could see what he was doing.

"I did not," Art replied.

"You're lying. No one else has access to my terminal."

"It is not in my programing to lie. I may withhold information, but I cannot lie."

"And we're just supposed to take your word for it?" Jacob snorted.

Henry rubbed at his temple and let out a loud sigh. "This is getting us nowhere. Let's go have a talk with Gaël. This falls under the I.T. security officer's purview, yes?" When Jacob nodded, Henry continued. "He'll be able to confirm or deny Kal… I mean Art's assessment. It's a waste of time to keep arguing amongst ourselves."

Jacob turned on his heel and stormed out without another word. The door slammed behind him, and all the tension seemed to dissipate with his abrupt departure. I was left feeling almost out of breath, as though I was caught in a whirlwind that had sucked the air from my lungs. I forced myself to inhale slow and deep. I realized my muscles were taut and consciously let them relax.

Henry unclenched his fists and shook them out a little before turning to me. "Why don't you two go grab some breakfast? There's no reason we should all get dragged down this rabbit hole. I'll catch up with you after we get it straightened out."

"Are you sure?" I asked.

Becca shoved me toward the door. "He's sure. Let's go, I'm starving. And you know how I get when I'm hungry."

Henry smiled and winked at me. "Mort could use some breakfast, too."

His soft chuckle broke any last vestige of apprehension I was feeling, and I reached out to playfully push his bare shoulder. The sensation of his warm skin left me feeling like I was some sort of a flirting genius. I lifted a shoulder to my chin and looked at him through half-closed eyes in an attempt to be sultry. As I turned, I smiled coyly over my shoulder and followed Becca out of the room. I never made it to the door. Only a few steps into my seduction and I fell over the coffee table. My shins collided with the edge, and momentum carried the top half of my body forward. I landed face first on the glass, with no time to even pray that it would hold my weight without shattering. My heels came up behind me and caught the front of one of the leather chairs, sending it tipping backwards almost on top of Mort.

I jumped up quickly, ignoring the throbbing in my shins and dragged Becca the rest of the way to the hall. I yelled something that was most likely gibberish and rushed off in search of the elevator George mentioned the day before.

We followed the hall and soon found ourselves in front of a pair of silver, sliding doors set into the rock wall of an otherwise dead end. Before either of us could speak, the doors slid open in one smooth motion. We clambered inside and turned just in time to watch the doors close with a quiet swoosh. I took deep breaths while I rubbed my sore legs.

"Where are the buttons?" Becca pondered.

I looked up through a curtain of hair, grateful that she was ignoring what just transpired. "They have to be here somewhere, unless the elevator can read our minds and knows we want to go to the top floor," I joked.

The lurch in my stomach told me we were moving. The give in my knees indicated we were moving up.

Becca's eyes went wide. She moved a hand to cover her head. I frowned at her and studied the walls around us.

"It can't really read your mind, Becks."

Her cheeks reddened, and she quickly lowered her hand.

We both jumped a bit when the doors split open, revealing Jacob and another man huddled on the other side.

"If that information got into the wrong hands—" Jacob's voice was low and rushed, but he quieted completely when he noticed the elevator wasn't empty.

The other man only looked up once Jacob was done talking.

Jacob held a hand up to stop the other man from following him onto the elevator. "Go take care of it," he barked, and the man scooted off.

"I'll call you shortly to make sure it's done!" Jacob shouted before the doors closed off his words. "Ladies." He didn't even bother turning to address us; he just stared at the closed doors.

We stood there for an awkward moment. He finally turned, a confused frown on his face. "Why aren't we moving? Aren't you going up to breakfast?" Without waiting for a reply he called out, "Top floor."

The lurch in my stomach and bend in my knees reoccured. The light went on in Becca's eyes just as the realization hit me. *Voice activated.* But we both kept quiet about our revelation as we rose up through the volcano.

I longed for cheesy elevator music as the silence grew uncomfortably thick. Our arrival couldn't come fast enough, but we still waited to let Jacob off first. He made no move to be chivalrous, stomped out in front of us, and disappeared into the crowded cafeteria.

"Well, that was unpleasant," Becca said, unnecessarily.

I nodded. "Let's go get some grub." I linked arms with her, and we joined the line to walk through the buffet style kitchen.

We filled up our plates with pungent fruits, steaming, eggless pancakes, and French toast sprinkled with powdered sugar.

"Sorry, we're out of whipped cream," one of the kitchen staff informed us as we drenched our cakes and toast in sticky, delicious maple syrup. "We only have a few cows, and we don't push their milk production, so when we run out, we run out."

"That's okay," I replied and shoved a disappointed Becca toward the tables and benches set up nearby.

We finished our breakfast in the comfortable silence that is built upon years of friendship. Becca used her spoon to move around the remaining pulp in her grapefruit bowl. My quick intake of breath must have been audible, because from the corner of my eye her head jerked up. Her gaze followed mine to watch Henry and Lips enter the mess hall. They were followed closely by a man I didn't recognize.

I may or may not have let out a quiet growl as I watched Lips all but drape herself over Henry.

"You need to stop spending so much time with animals," Becca smirked.

"What?" I gave her my best innocent look.

She just went back to playing with her breakfast. Henry gracefully maneuvered onto the bench next to me, making it look so easy. Instead of sitting across from us, Lips scooted in on the other side of him, forcefully bumping us down the bench to the point where I almost fell off the end. I couldn't see her with Henry's large frame between us, but I noticed the mean-girl look Becca gave her on my behalf and felt vindicated.

The man who had accompanied them into the room stood awkwardly for a moment, wringing his hands. Then, after careful consideration, and perhaps a mental pep talk, he took a seat on the bench next to Becca. They smiled shyly at each other and proceeded to act like the other person didn't exist.

Henry turned to me. "I'm sure you remember Kalypso from yesterday."

"I told you to call me Lips. We're friends now," she purred.

We were packed so closely on the bench that I could tell Lips had leaned into him as she said it. I resisted the urge to reach around Henry and shove her right off the seat.

Henry didn't miss a beat. "But you haven't met Gaël yet. He's the Chief Security Officer here on the island, though his focus is on IT security."

Gaël's light-brown cheeks reddened. He smiled but kept his brown eyes focused on a spot on the table in front of him.

"I'm Kaly," I said, reaching out a hand.

"Rhymes with pal-ee," he said softly. His eyes darted up to mine and then back to the table. "Sorry, I'm bad with names, so I try to come up with ways to help me remember them."

He slowly lifted his eyes to look at Becca. She turned a

little so she could shake his hand as well.

"I'm Becca, nice to meet you."

Gaël's lips moved, but no sound came out. His eyes darted back to the spot on the table. "Nice to meet you, too," he stated, once he'd cleared his throat.

After an uncomfortable lull, I nudged Henry and whispered, "Did you get everything straightened out?"

He opened his mouth to respond but was interrupted by Jacob, who yelled across the crowded mess hall.

"Lips!"

Everyone in the room grew silent and watched the argument unfold.

"Lips! You forgot to turn off the cell jammer." Jacob's hands were pressed into the sides of his wide hips. "Again!"

Instead of going over to talk to him, Lips just shouted back from where she was sitting. "So what?"

"So how are we supposed to call anyone," for some reason Jacob pointed his wrist and continued, "if all cell signals are jammed?"

Henry leaned away from Lips as the bickering continued. It gave me a clear line of sight to watch her roll her eyes. "Use the house phones. That's what they're there for!"

"I'm just supposed to know what landline everyone is closest to at all times? No! So then what, I'm supposed to hoof it all over the blasted facility looking for the person I need to talk to?"

Lips' smile turned nasty. "Consider it a favor, Jacob. I'm just trying to look out for your health. Goodness knows you could stand to get more exercise."

There were some snickers from around the room.

Jacob's face nearly turned purple. "Maybe if you spent more time worrying about your job and less time worrying about judging other people, we wouldn't keep having this problem!"

Henry stood and placed a hand on Lips' shoulder before she could call out any further retort. "That sounds like it covers the topic at hand. I think if you two have anything further to discuss, it would be best if you did so in private."

Anger flashed across Lips' face, but she recovered quickly with a sickly sweet smile. "Of course, Henry. You're right. I'll go flip the jammer so poor Jacob doesn't have a heart attack trying to find anyone."

She squeezed Henry's hand and then stood from her place at the table. She slid out from behind the bench and stalked off toward the elevator, leaving her dirty dishes behind. Gaël's brows furrowed, and his mouth drew down unhappily at the corners. He quickly scooped up her tray and chased after Lips. I watched with growing admiration as he shoved the tray at her and gave her quite an earful.

I didn't notice George had come up behind me until he cleared his throat politely. He leaned in to address me. "Gaël gets a little upset when people don't clean up after themselves. He thinks it's disrespectful to the people who work so hard to run the mess hall."

From across the table, Becca chimed in, "Gaël is right."

George smiled and continued. "What is it he's always saying? 'If you want to see the true measure of a man, watch how he treats his inferiors, not his equals.'"

"J.K. Rowling," Becca practically shouted.

George took a quick step back. "Excuse me?"

"It's a quote by J.K. Rowling! I love that quote," she gushed.

George looked at me, his mouth dropped open with his silent question.

I chuckled. "Becca is a huge fan. Rowling wrote the *Harry Potter* series," I explained.

"Oh, yes, yes, of course," George replied. "I just assumed it was Gaël's words of wisdom. Ah well, I came by to fetch you so we could finish our tour of the facility. I'm sure today's exploration will be of great interest to *you*." He pointed at me and then spun around without waiting for a response. "Don't forget your trays," he called out jovially.

Becca shrugged and got up. Henry stood and helped us gather our trays. We were all careful to pick up after ourselves before leaving the table.

"I'll catch up with you later," Henry murmured in my ear.

I nodded numbly, afraid to try to speak with his hand planted warmly on my lower back.

Becca threaded her arm into mine and led me after George. A stupid grin won against my attempts to fight it and spread across my face.

"So, Gaël seemed… interesting?" Becca said.

"Mmm hmm." I couldn't think of anything other than where my back still tingled.

I followed Becca and George to the lift. Certain that

nothing could interest me more than the man I had left my whole life behind for.

But events were about to prove me wrong. So very, very wrong.

Chapter 4

We hadn't made it far from the elevator when squealing noises grew so loud I was certain the world was about to come to an end. Frantic shouts punctured the animalistic cacophony but not enough that I could make out any of their words. Not that it would have mattered. Even if I had been able to understand what was being said, it couldn't possibly have prepared me for what was coming.

In all my years of working with animals, I had never come across an angrier herd than the one that flew around the corner and rushed down the hallway in our direction.

"Oh my god!" George shouted.

He and Becca split off in opposite directions to hug the walls. I wasn't so quick, and hadn't quite made it out of their path when the first pig raced by me. His wide body struck my legs with enough force to knock me down. I had to pull myself out of the way with my hands and arms, as my legs were trampled by stampeding hooves.

After reaching the relative safety of the hallway's edge, I curled into the fetal position. Soon the the last of the pigs had run by, but I didn't loosen my grip, even as the noise faded with distance.

"What was that!" Becca demanded as she rushed to my side.

George was staring after the pigs and was shaking his head in wide-eyed disbelief. "I have no idea. I didn't know pigs did anything like that."

"They don't," I mumbled, as I buried my face into my aching legs. "Not unless something hurt or scared them… a lot."

"That can't be," George's voice trailed off.

"Well, obviously it can," Becca added unnecessarily. "Kaly, are you okay?"

I winced as I finally stretched out my legs. They were sore, and I couldn't keep them from shaking. "I don't think anything's broken. But they hurt pretty bad."

George paced back and forth and scratched at the back of his neck, just below the hairline. "This doesn't make any sense. No one here would scare or hurt them. This doesn't make any sense."

"You said that already," I growled through clenched teeth.

Becca pulled up my semi-shredded pant legs to better examine the damage. Hoof-shaped bruises were already starting to form. A couple places were bleeding from where my skin was deeply gouged.

George wandered over but continued to stare in the direction the pigs had fled, phone in hand. His back was to us, but I heard the unmistakable, obnoxious tone of no service warble loudly in the now-quiet hall.

"Lips forgot to turn off the cell jammer," Becca reminded him.

George cursed under his breath and suddenly took off.

"Wait!" Becca called after him. "Where are you going?"

"I have to get to a phone. Security needs to know about this right away. If you need the infirmary, you can take the elevator all the way down. It's the whole bottom floor; you can't miss it." Then he disappeared around the corner.

Becca blew a chunk of her hair out of her face. She typically only did so when she was angry but was trying to keep her cool.

"I'll be all right." I tried to help defuse the situation.

"I can't believe he just took off like that!" Her voice shook a little.

"He's right, security needs to know about this so they can get a handle on the situation before someone else gets hurt."

She held her hands out to me. "Can you stand? We should get you to a doctor."

I let her pull me up, trying not to grimace too hard when I put weight on my battered legs. "I'd like to know what caused the stampede, too. I wonder if they have video surveillance. We could see what happened to make them react like that."

Becca watched me hobble in the direction of the elevator, hovering just within arm's reach, offering a steadying hand any time I teetered.

I batted her hands away. "I'm fine, I've got this. I'm just a little sore, but I'll be okay."

It was slow going to the infirmary. I tried to play it off like I was all right, but the pain kept me from walking at a decent pace.

The introduction with Dr. Yates was brief. And the look on her face made the trip worth it, as I explained what happened. I could see her struggling with how to process the fact that I had been trampled by stampeding pigs while she gave me a cursory examination.

"I used to work the ER on the South Side of Chicago." She laughed humorlessly as she checked my vitals and monitored my reaction to the painkillers she'd administered. "And I think I can safely say, this is the weirdest thing I've ever seen."

The drugs worked deliciously fast. I smiled at her, happily enjoying the euphoria of being pain free. "I doubt they have many pigs living in Chicago."

The doctor's eyes widened. "No, no they don't. The only ones I ever saw were already in the form of bacon or chops. Do pigs often stampede like that?"

I snorted and then scratched at my nose. A side effect of the drugs—they made my nose itch. "No, no they don't." I laughed at my clever use of her own phrase.

Becca rolled her eyes. "Sorry, she's not usually like this."

"Don't apologize for me!" I protested.

"Shhh, you're being weird."

"You're always weird, but I don't shush you."

Becca's lips twitched at the corners.

The doctor chuckled. "It's okay. I gave her a strong pain reliever. Sometimes it makes people a bit loopy. I'm used to it."

"But not to rampaging pigs!" I shouted and then fell into a fit of giggles.

After my wounds were thoroughly cleaned, the doctor leaned in to examine my legs. "Looks like you're going to need a few stitches."

Henry came rushing into the infirmary as the doctor prepared a suture kit. "Kaly!" He called from across the room. "I came as soon as I heard! Are you okay?"

"Oh, this should be interesting." Becca smirked.

"Heeeeeeeey, beautiful," I said, making finger guns in his direction. "Oh wait, you're not beautiful, *I'm* beautiful. So *you* should be handsome. Heeeeeeeey, handsome."

His steps faltered a bit. His brow sank, and he smiled at the same time. "Um, hey?"

"You mean 'hey beautiful,' remember? I'm beautiful because I'm a girl and you're handsome because you're a boy." I gave him my most winning smile.

Becca smothered her laugh behind a fake cough.

"What's going on?" Henry asked her.

"Kaly was given some potent drugs. She's feeling pretty good right now," Becca explained.

Realization sparked in his deep, blue eyes and his smile made me tingle as much as the medication did.

"Is she okay?" He reached out to grab my hand.

"Yeah, she needs a few stitches, but she'll be fine," Yates answered.

I stared down at our entwined hands. I marveled at the way our fingers fit so well together, like they were made just for this. His grip was strong but gentle, and I never wanted to let go. I left it there as long as I could before I had to itch my nose again, only realizing days later that I had another hand I could have used.

The doctor finished stitching me up.

"Only six," I said proudly. "Nowhere near my record. Told ya I was fine."

"Yes," Becca responded in a placating tone. "You were right. But how about we get you to bed for a bit so you can rest?"

I tried to protest, but Henry cut me off. "It'll help keep the swelling down, right, Doc?"

Dr. Yates looked up from the electronic tablet she was tapping notes into. "What? Oh, yes, rest would be good."

"I'm perfectly fine." I tried to stand up, but my legs wobbled traitorously beneath me.

Without a second thought, Henry carefully scooped me up in his arms and carried me back toward the elevator.

"We have a wheelchair you can use," the doctor called after us.

"No, thank you." I waved her off over Henry's muscular shoulder. "I prefer to ride Henry."

Becca snorted somewhere behind us. My head rested against Henry's chest and I could feel him shake with silent laughter. I tried to figure out what was so funny but soon gave up. Exhaustion was calling me, so I let Henry's steady heartbeat lull me to sleep.

When I came to, I felt groggy and disoriented. It took me a moment to remember where I was. My new room still felt so unfamiliar. The curtains were drawn, but light still tried to force its way inside. I sat up and placed my feet on the heated tile floor, then waited for the room to stop spinning. When I was finally able to stand, I stifled a cry as pain shot up my legs. I took a few tentative steps, and the intense aching slowly subsided to more of a dull throbbing. I heard low, muffled voices coming from the next room, so I limped to the door and cracked it open.

"If you ask me, it was a distraction," Gaël was saying.

"But a distraction from what?" Henry muttered, running a hand through his short, dark hair, leaving it rumpled but in an attractive way.

Gaël traced his finger along the surface of the coffee table. "I'm running diagnostics, but I'm not finding anything unusual. Your AI said it discovered more gaps and thinks something else was removed."

Henry leaned forward in his seat. "You mean removed like Jacob's files were removed?"

Gaël nodded.

"What were the files?"

Gaël shrugged. "We won't know until someone reports them missing. Even your AI couldn't tell what they were."

"You can call him Art."

Gaël looked confused, so Henry quickly elaborated. "The AI has chosen to name itself Art. You can call him Art instead of 'the AI.'"

"Oh, okay. Well… Art wasn't able to determine what was taken, only that more files were removed. I'm trying to find out. I've asked everyone to go through all their research."

"But it's a completely closed system here, isn't it?" Henry's knee started bouncing as he spoke.

Gaël seemed to follow Henry's logic. "Which means whoever removed the files has to be on the island."

"But that still doesn't explain the pigs," I said, as I finally moved out from the doorway.

Henry and Gaël both glanced up in surprise.

"Kaly, you're awake." Henry jumped up and hurried to my side.

He helped me to the couch and sat down gently beside me, his eyes assessed my legs before returning to meet my gaze.

I pressed the question again. "So what were the pigs a distraction from? It seems like overkill just to take some files."

The two men exchanged a look I couldn't decipher.

"We don't know," Gaël answered.

"Yet," Henry added resolutely.

The door to the hallway banged open, causing me to jump and then wince from the pain of the sudden movement.

"Could someone give me a hand?" Becca mumbled around a paper bag she had clenched in her teeth. She entered the room with a tray balanced precariously in one hand, and her other arm was wrapped around a box that wafted steam from the top. The aroma drifting in with her was heavenly. My stomach rumbled its appreciation, and my keen sense of smell picked out hints of tomato sauce under the overwhelming scent of garlic.

Gaël practically dove over his seat to get to her. He

relieved her of the tray and the bag and then stood waiting for further instructions. Becca stretched out her jaw a little as she maneuvered around the living room furniture to the small wooden table. Our conversation all but forgotten, Gaël followed behind her like a happy little puppy and let her boss him around as they arranged the food across the table.

"Dinner's ready!" she announced cheerfully.

"Dinner?" I balked. "What happened to lunch?"

Henry patted my hand. "You were out for a while. We thought it best to let you sleep. George is still working with a crew to get everything back in order, so the rest of the tour will have to wait till tomorrow."

"*If* you're feeling up to it," Becca interjected. "You can take another day to rest if you want, Kaly."

Henry helped pull me up from the couch, and I shuffled over to the table. "Tomorrow is fine. I'd really like to see the rest of the facility. Especially since George made a point of saying there's a part I'd be especially interested in."

Henry pulled a chair out and helped me ease into it. I watched out of the corner of my eye as Gaël did the same for Becca.

"You're a veterinarian right?" Gaël inquired.

I nodded.

Gaël smiled shyly at me. "He probably wants to show you The Sanctum."

My growling stomach pushed me past polite decorum, and I scooped some noodles and sauce onto my plate. "What's The Sanctum?"

"Oh, I won't ruin the surprise." He smiled mischievously.

"It's better if you see it. Words don't do it justice."

"I'm starting to think it doesn't exist." I laughed. "Everyone keeps saying how much I'm going to like it, but then we don't actually make it there."

"I'd take you myself, but they prefer that I stay out of there." Gaël smiled sheepishly.

"How come?" Becca asked.

"It's a long story. I'll tell you after you've seen it." Gaël grabbed a roll and passed the basket to me.

"So I guess I'll never hear the story then?" I quipped.

Gaël smirked. "Guess not."

I tossed my roll at him, which he caught with one hand. The laughter came easily after that, and so did the conversation. We talked about everything from what life was like on the island for Gaël, to what happened to bring Becca and I here. The simulated windows slowly darkened, and soon stars twinkled pleasantly in between scattered clouds as the night went on.

Every now and then, I peppered in a question or comment about The Sanctum to try to glean more information, but Gaël was too clever and never let anything slip. My curiosity was definitely piqued, but my frustration was kept at bay with Gaël's hilarious jokes and Henry's thought-provoking topics, like the advancement of human civilization. We discussed Art and what his technology would mean to the world. If Art was listening, he never joined the conversation, though I couldn't help but wonder what he'd say if we asked him.

The late hour combined with the heavy meal took its toll.

Yawning grew frequent, and at long last Henry suggested cleaning up and heading to bed. Becca gave him a grateful look. I knew she was thinking about how tired she was, but that she didn't want to be the one to suggest leaving. Being her best friend for so many years, I could recognize when she was interested in a guy. And all the signs now pointed to her attraction to Gaël.

We said our goodnights and Mort dutifully followed me to my room. I fell asleep with a smile, thinking about how happy my best friend seemed and how tomorrow I would get to see The Sanctum. It was going to be a great day, I could feel it.

I woke with a stretch and immediately regretted it. Pain receptors in my legs screamed frantic messages to my brain in response to the movement. I lay still and breathed through the pain. That's when I realized something was off; it was too quiet. I lifted my head and looked around the room for Mort. Panic set in when I didn't see him. Sitting up quickly was a mistake; the stabbing ache brought tears to my eyes. I took Lamaze breaths and tried to figure out my next move. That's when I spied the note on the bedside table; it had my name on it.

> *Brought you some painkillers. They are on the shelf above the sink in your bathroom. Mort finally decided to spend some quality time with me, so don't panic that he's not here. I'll see you at breakfast.*
> *~ H ~*

Slowly rolling out of bed, I was careful not to jar my throbbing lower limbs when I finally placed my feet on the floor. Grunting like a tennis player, I exerted enough force to get myself into a standing position and turned in the direction of the bathroom.

"It's just a few steps." I tried to psych myself up enough to get moving.

I took my time crossing the bedroom to the on-suite bathroom. The pills waited right where Henry said they'd be. After dumping two into my hand, I popped them in my mouth. They were large and hard to swallow; it took a couple tries to get them down.

My legs just needed to loosen up a bit, but I didn't want to be the one to have to loosen them—at least not until the medication kicked in. So I stood in the shower for longer than usual and let the warm water seep into my skin. The heat worked its magic on my overly tight muscles, and, combined with the effects of the pills, I was soon feeling awesome.

I rummaged through the drawers of my room, grateful that Becca had not only located our luggage but also unpacked my stuff for me. And like a true best friend, there was a variety of my favorite clothes. She knew me so well. I pulled out a pair of khaki cargo pants softened by frequent use and a black t-shirt that I knew fit me in a flattering way. The laces on my work boots were a little stiff from disuse but held their knots as I set out to find Becca and Henry. I don't know what made her think to pack these, but they were probably the best option for the island.

I found the common room empty. The door to Henry's room was open, but Becca's door was still closed. I scanned Henry's room as I made my way across the common area. Empty. My thoughts wandered to where he might be as I knocked a quick staccato on Becca's door.

"Who is it?" she called out from somewhere inside.

"It's Kaly."

"You're up early." The door did nothing to muffle her snark. "Give me a minute. I'm almost ready, and then we can grab some breakfast."

"Okay." I went to the couch and contemplated sitting down. The medication was helping, but it was still hard for me to bend my legs. Instead I walked to the door that lead to the hallway. Pushing it open, I took a quick glance outside before leaning against the doorjamb to wait for Becca. A couple of women in lab coats walked past me and gave me a nod.

As I waited, my mind wandered to what I'd be doing if we were still back in Boston. I'd be working in my vet clinic, probably performing yet another spay or neuter that made up a large chunk of my business. And being here was definitely more exciting that diagnosing obesity in yet another pug or golden retriever.

But how long would our stay on Nowhere Island last? Henry made it seem like we would be here for a while, staying just out of Pastern's reach. I hoped Jenny, my office administrator, was handling things back in Boston. My lawyer handled all the paperwork to make her a partner in my clinic; I hoped that would be enough to motivate her to hold down the fort in my absence. If anyone could keep the other employees and doctors in line while I was gone, it was Jenny.

These mundane details were once again crowded out by the more exciting ones and my mind turned back to Pastern. It was still hard to believe that some multi-billion dollar company was after me and my best friend. Then again, after finding alien artificial intelligence, even the weirdest things seemed normal by comparison. Pastern wouldn't stop until they got their hands on Art's technology, which made the length of our stay here uncertain. But I needed to remain positive; there were worse places we could be stuck.

"Okay, I'm ready," Becca announced, startling me out of my thoughts.

"Great, let's—"

A man with soft brown eyes and a bright, white smile was coming down the hall and calling my name.

"Dr. Aiton. Kaly Aiton?" His gaze bounced from me to Becca and back again.

"Um, that's me," I responded. "Do we know each other?"

His warm eyes locked onto mine. "No, but George mentioned you were a veterinarian. I was hoping you could give me a hand."

"He may have mentioned you, but I don't know your name. Nor did he mention that you'd be coming to see me."

"The name's Ross Sotirios. Perhaps you've heard of me? My dashing good looks and my roguish ways? My buddy, George, loves me. I'm sure he mentioned me *ad nauseam*."

"He mentioned you were responsible for Lucky and not

doing a very good job of it. That's about it."

He chuckled; a gentle, friendly sound that settled my initial unease. "Well, he's not wrong. Lucky is a cheeky monkey."

Our rolling eyes made his smile widen.

"Speaking of cheeky monkeys, you must be Becca," Ross continued, holding out a hand to my friend.

Her cheeks reddened slightly, and Becca hesitantly offered him her hand. She sputtered a few incoherent words as he gently kissed the tops of her fingers.

"George didn't tell me much about you other than to mention your beauty," Ross said smoothly. "Though I don't think he did you justice."

Becca smiled nervously and looked at me with slight panic in her eyes. Ross kept his intense gaze on her face.

I cleared my throat and took a small step forward, placing myself slightly in front of Becca, forcing Ross to break his focus.

"So you said you needed a hand."

"Along with being a monkey wrangler," he wiggled his eyebrows playfully, "I'm also a researcher here on the island. But when I have some free time, I indulge a hobby of sorts."

"I'm almost afraid to ask," Becca scoffed.

"It's not entirely above board, but it's not creepy or anything." His smile turned mischievous. "Long story short, I've been liberating animals from testing facilities around the world. Saving them from a life of misery. Right now, I've got six beagles I'd really like you to examine for me."

"Beagles?" Becca's frown matched my own.

For the first time, his winning smile slipped from his face. "They're used a lot for testing. Their disposition is so sweet that even when they're hurt, they don't lash out. Sadly, it makes them perfect test subjects. Such kind animals, how could I not do something to save them? So I go in, rescue them, and take them to where I know they'll be safe and well treated."

I took a deep breath and let it out slowly. "Well, after all the work you put into getting them here, the least I can do is examine them. Where are they?"

His smile returned, and he put an arm around my shoulder. "Right this way, my dear. I'm so glad you've joined our merry bunch of misfits here on *Île de Nulle Part*."

Chapter 5

The room was cool and clinical, with stark-white walls. The floors were a smooth, light-colored concrete. Two shiny, steel examining tables sat just inside the door. Adjustable exam lights hung over both tables, their florescent glow reflected off the tables and onto the bare walls. Examination equipment rested on a darker metal cart nearby. My eyes quickly took all this in but then were drawn to the seven cages lining the other side of the room.

Weary eyes gazed forlornly in my direction from each medium-sized crate. I swallowed hard around the lump in my throat.

"Why are they still in the cages!" Becca demanded.

Ross gently touched her elbow. "They've spent their whole lives in those small prison cells. It takes a while to get them acclimated to freedom. We have to go slow; it helps with the rehabilitation. We'll get them checked out and then work on getting them out of those."

"I can't be here right now." Becca was near tears. "I'm going to go up and get some breakfast. Let me know when they're ready to come out of those horrible cages."

Before Ross or I could respond, she was gone.

"She eats when she's upset," I explained. "It's how she copes."

He looked skeptical but didn't say anything.

Taking a long, deep breath, I slowly eased toward the first crate. "Let's get this done so we can take these sweet babies out into some sunshine and fresh air."

I had done my share of euthanizing beloved pets. On many occasions, I delivered bad news to worried families. Far too often I performed surgeries that weren't enough. But this was by far the hardest thing I'd ever had to do. Thinking about what these poor dogs had suffered through, I had to stop a few times during the examinations as tears blurred my vision. Their cowering at my every touch wrecked me the most.

Once the exams were done, I was relieved to find that none of the dogs had any serious health issues, aside from some skin deterioration and signs of prolonged malnourishment. One of the older beagles had a heart murmur I'd have to keep an eye on, but as he most likely had it since birth and had lived this long already, I was confident he would be all right too. I applied a topical skin treatment to the lot of them, then filled their bowls with a protein-rich dog food from the storage room.

Ross helped me inject tracking chips between each dog's shoulder blades.

"We tag all the animals I rescue. We like to be able to keep an eye on them. I'll rustle up a laptop for you and show you how the tracking software works," he said when we were done.

"I should give Becca a call. She'll like helping with this next part. You were planning to let them out of their crates now, right?"

Ross nodded. "We've got this really nice grassy area that will be perfect for their first trip out. Right next to The Sanctum."

I pulled out my cell phone, relieved to see it still had some battery left.

Ross frowned and pointed at my phone. "That won't work."

I pulled up Becca's number and was about to hit dial. "It will, Lips finally turned the cell jammer off. Gaël mentioned it last night at dinner."

Ross gave me a curious look.

My cheeks flushed. "No, it wasn't like that. There were a bunch of us at dinner. Well, four of us…. I just…."

He held up his hands and laughed. "It's okay; Just giving you a hard time. You're easily flustered. It's really cute."

My face grew even hotter.

He plucked the phone out of my hand and waved it in the air. "But this phone still won't work, only ones made specifically for our network."

"Then why the jammer?"

"Technically Satphones will work here, too, but for the most part they aren't allowed. So no one really has 'em here."

"Unless you're a pirate." I couldn't help but smile at the word.

He laughed. "I heard we had an exciting visit the day you arrived. Was that your first encounter with real-life pirates?"

I waved him off. "Naw, I spent some time on the lawless waters of the Caribbean. Some pretty nefarious scoundrels around those parts."

He gave a polite chuckle that came a moment too late.

I pressed on quickly, trying to get away from my bad joke. "What if I snuck a satellite phone onto the island?"

"You couldn't. We are extremely thorough in our searches before you even get close to the island. Only authorized personnel are allowed to have them."

"Wait, someone searched my stuff?" I couldn't conceal the horrified look on my face. "When? On the plane?"

Ross shrugged, his expression seemed apologetic, but he didn't apologize. "And even if you managed to get one here somehow, the second you turn it on, it will light up their sensors like a Christmas tree. They'll kick on the jammer faster than you can say 'Can you hear me now?'"

I wrapped my arms around my body, hugging myself at the thought of someone searching my things. "So I guess I'm going to need one of those network phones then?"

"We can make that happen." He pulled one of my hands loose and draped it in the crook of his arm, then led me out of the room. "Let's go see if we can track down your friend the old-fashioned way. What ever did we do before cell phones?"

We found Becca back in our common room.

"Hey, we're done with the exams. The dogs are good to go. We're ready to start acclimating them to a new life of freedom. Figured you'd like to be there for that part," I said as I made my way through to my room.

I needed to grab some more painkillers; the ones from this morning had worn off, and my legs were throbbing with each step.

"Now you're talking!" she called from the other room as I filled a cup in my bathroom sink.

My stomach rumbled loudly. "I need food first."

"If you are going to get something to eat," Ross said loudly, "I have some things I need to take care of. I'll meet you back in the examine room in, let's say, an hour?"

"Sounds good." I re-entered the common room and he was already gone. I shrugged and turned to Becca. "It's past lunch time, and I missed breakfast. I'm starving!"

"I was going to bring you something to eat but I got… um… sidetracked," Becca mumbled.

"By anyone I know?" I smiled conspiratorially at her.

"Shut up." She laughed and threw one of the pillows from the couch at me. "Don't make me recount the side-tracker who brought us to this island."

I threw the cushion back at her. "Yeah, yeah, let's go."

Becca and I scanned the crowded mess hall as we balanced our trays of food.

"There!" Her hands were full, so Becca jutted her chin to point.

I followed the general direction of her chin and finally saw what she meant. Henry was sitting at a table with George and Gaël, and there appeared to be a couple open seats. We wove our way through the crowd. I nearly dropped my tray twice but somehow managed to save it both times. Luckily the men were in deep conversation and didn't notice our approach or my near misses with catastrophe.

"It's rather odd that no one has been able to find the missing files." Gaël prodded the corn suspended in his chowder.

"So either the files aren't missing and Art is wrong, or—" Henry began.

And George finished his sentence. "Or someone is lying."

I sat in the empty seat next to Henry, and Becca squeezed into the open space between Gaël and George.

"Why would someone lie about the missing files?" I ventured into their conversation.

The three guys all jumped a little at the sound of my voice.

"Sorry," I apologized with a small smile. "Didn't think you were having a private conversation in the middle of a crowded dining hall."

My joke fell a little flat, but Henry smiled politely anyway.

"No, it's all right. Join us. It's not private." He placed his hand on my knee for a moment before continuing. "We were just trying to figure out Art's latest mystery."

"And not having much luck," Gaël added, smiling sweetly at Becca.

A loud thumping noise interrupted Gaël's next statement, like the sound a microphone makes when someone taps it. A three-tone chime sounded overhead, and the room fell quiet. Lips' voice blared from speakers on the ceiling.

"This is a reminder that tomorrow is the supply run. Please have all acquisition forms in no later than 6:00 p.m.. Any requests over three thousand must be pre-approved by a member of the governing board."

Someone groaned loudly at the table behind me.

"Why does she always have to go through this every time?" A man whined.

Gaël responded. "It's protocol, Theo. You should try sticking to it sometime, might change your life."

Theo was about to respond when Henry turned in his seat to glare at the protocol infringer; it was enough to shut Theo up.

We resumed our lunches, and Gaël leaned in to talk to Henry. "I'm going to go with you tomorrow on the supply run if that's okay?"

"Sure," Henry said around the bite of coconut curry he had just crammed in his mouth.

There was something comforting about the way Henry talked with his mouth full. It meant he was less perfect than he seemed. Maybe he wasn't so far out of my league after all.

"But if you need something, I don't mind picking it up for you." Little bits of food flew out as Henry spoke.

I stifled a giggle when I saw the face Becca made.

Gaël leaned even further across the table and whispered, "I've been discussing with Art how I might set up a snare on our network. So if anyone steals more files we can catch them. But I need to pick up some things. I thought I'd go myself so I don't have to complete a requisition form. I doubt anyone will be able to tell what what I'm planning, but if they were smart enough to get those files the way they did, they might be smart enough to figure out what I'm trying to do. Better safe than sorry."

Henry nodded and continued munching his curry.

"Wait, you're going for supplies tomorrow?" Becca's eyes widened and she rushed on quickly. "That sounds suspiciously like shopping. I didn't have much time to pack and there's a bunch of stuff I really need. Can I go with you?"

I jumped in, "Oh, that's a good idea! Can I come too?"

"Actually, I was going to ask if you two would like to do just that." Henry leaned in to nudge me with his shoulder.

"Great, I'm woefully unprepared for an extended stay." I leaned over to nudge him back.

"Excuuuuse me," Becca glowered. "I did the best I could with the short time I had to prepare."

"Of course, you did a fantastic job." I reached out to put a reassuring hand on her arm, but instead I knocked over two glasses of apple juice and a bowl of bean-and-barley soup.

Our small lunch group leapt up at once and began dabbing at the mess with all the napkins we could get our hands on.

"Am I too late for the party?" Ross quipped, coming up to stand by our table.

"No, just Kaly being Kaly." Becca groaned and loaded up a tray with our used napkins and other soaked garbage.

"Okay." Ross stepped aside to allow Becca room to get past him with her overflowing tray. "I came to see if you were ready to go." He winked at me.

Henry put his hand on my lower back before addressing Ross. "I'm sorry, I don't think we've had the pleasure of an introduction. I'm Henry, and you are?"

Ross' eyes flicked down to Henry's hand on my back. He gave his winning smile and then gave Henry a mock salute. "I'm Ross. It's so nice to finally meet you."

"You and Kaly know each other?"

"George told me she might be able to take a look at the beagles I rescued."

"I see." Henry leaned in and I thought he was going to whisper something to me, so I leaned in as well.

His words were anything but a whisper. "I was hoping you'd join me for dinner tonight? I have something special in mind. Meet you in our common room around 6:30?" His words were for me but his eyes held Ross' gaze.

Ross' smile never faltered. Ignoring Henry's death glare, he brazenly turned to me and said, "Ready love?"

"Becca's coming too," I blurted out.

Henry gave me a look I couldn't decipher.

I placed a hand on his chest and tried to remember how to speak English. "I would have to love dinner." Mentally composing myself, I tried again. "I mean, would love to *have* dinner."

Henry's smile returned, and I couldn't help but melt a little.

"I'll see you later." He beamed.

I didn't trust myself to say anything intelligent, so I just nodded and made a beeline for the elevator. Grabbing

Becca's elbow, I hauled her along on my hasty exit and didn't dare looking back.

At the far end of the exam room was a door leading outside. We carried all seven crates out and into a small, grassy area. Bushes formed a natural barrier that made it an ideal place to release the poor creatures for their first steps outside.

"They're so quiet," Becca murmured as we slowly opened each cage door.

Her statement hit me like a punch to the stomach. I had been so wrapped up in my examinations and trying not to think of the horrors these sweet babies had been through, I didn't even take note of the fact none of them made a peep.

Ross clenched his fists. "They call it 'de-barking,' and it's an atrocious practice. Heaven forbid those researches should have to listen to the howls and barking while doing their cruel experiments."

"I think I'm going to be sick." Becca covered her mouth.

"Come on sweet angel, it's okay. You're safe now." I tried to coax the nearest beagle from the only life he'd known.

It took about twenty minutes to get the first dog out onto the grass. Her bravery spurred the others on to make their own first steps of freedom. To watch them discover the joys of being regular dogs brought tears to my eyes. I stopped trying to fight it and just let them fall. We showered the seven courageous souls with kind words, yummy treats, and lots of gentle belly rubs.

"So what happens now?" Becca asked as she snuggled one of the older beagles.

"We'll introduce them to the other dogs on the island and make sure they get on okay. The ones who don't do well with the others will be brought back to the States and adopted by families that can care for them."

"Isn't it a bit much to bring them here just to take them back to the States?" She frowned.

Ross handed a treat to a particularly spunky boy and chuckled as the playful pup bounded off to join his new friends. "We don't bring them to the island if we can help it. But there were some complications with this rescue, so it was safest to bring them here."

"Complications?"

"It's best if you don't know the details." He smiled at her with a devilish grin.

The door from the examination room opened, and two women in purple lab coats came squealing out to join us.

"Ivy, Ainsley so glad you could come!" Ross called out, gently scooping up a shy beagle as he walked over to the newcomers.

The two ladies giggled and rushed to meet him. They cooed and nuzzled the dog in Ross' arms.

"We heard you were back and you brought puppies with you. We thought you might want some help with them," one of the women said in a sing-song voice.

"I would never turn down the help of two gorgeous ladies." He carefully handed over the dog.

The two women squealed some more and fawned over the precious pup. Becca caught my eye and pantomimed a gagging motion. I laughed and turned back to watch the rest of the beagle clan frolic together in utter bliss.

"Oh," the second woman called out, "George asked you to call him."

Ross gave her an enigmatic smile and pretended to tip an imaginary hat. "Excuse me for a moment, ladies," he said to us.

He wandered off, and I resumed watching the dogs roll and play in the grass. Ross was back by my side a few moments later, standing a little closer than was socially acceptable. "George was looking for you. Said he has some time and would like to finish giving you the tour. You still haven't seen The Sanctum?"

I shook my head.

He frowned. "That's weird. I figured that'd be the first place he took you."

"Why, what is it? I keep hearing about it but no one will tell me what it is," I groaned.

"It's a super-secret vault with all the proof of alien life that the government has been trying to hide, isn't it?" Becca guessed.

Ross gave us an impish grin and wiggled his eyebrows. "You'll have to wait and see."

"Ugh!" I grumbled. "Everyone keeps saying that. I'm starting to think it doesn't really exist."

"Oh, it exists, and you'll really find it of interest," he assured me.

"Yeah, yeah, everyone keeps saying that, too."

Becca gave me a playful shove. "And by everyone she means George and Gaël."

I made a face at her.

"We'll keep these guys and gals here tonight and then introduce them to the other dogs in the morning. If you're available, it'd be great if you could be here to help out." Ross placed his hand on my shoulder and gave a gentle squeeze.

"Sounds like a plan," I agreed. "Are you sure you don't need me to stay now?" I knelt down to scratch the ears of the closest beagle.

Ross nodded at the two women in lab coats. "I'll be fine. I've got some help. And word spreads pretty quick around here. Ainsley and Ivy aren't the only animal lovers on the island. I'm sure I'll be getting more help soon."

No sooner had he mentioned it, than the door opened and another man and woman in navy lab coats came through the door from the exam room.

Becca and I said our goodbyes to the dogs and decided to go back inside to wait for George.

"Nine o'clock tomorrow morning," Ross called after us. "See you then!" And he was back talking to Ivy and Ainsley before the door even closed behind us.

We didn't have to wait long; George soon came barreling into the room.

"Ah, here you are," he said, as though we were playing a game of hide-and-seek and he had finally discovered our hiding spot. "Are you ready to see it? I know I've been promising to show you since your arrival. The time has come! If you'll follow me, I'll take you to see The Sanctum."

Without a second glance, he took off down the hall. Becca shrugged and followed after him, trying to keep up with his quick pace. I was going to call to him and ask him to slow down but thought better of it. I didn't want to jinx it and miss my opportunity to finally see what all the fuss was about. So I kept my mouth shut and raced after them.

Chapter 6

"The moment you've been waiting for. Here it is, The Sanctum!"

George threw open a set of heavy double doors, and a blast of humid, sweet air washed over me. I could feel his eyes on me as I took in my surroundings. Lush trees and vegetation grew up to towering heights all around. When the doors closed behind us, it was like they disappeared. The entrance was now hidden by thick vines and flowers the size of my head.

I could hear a waterfall somewhere close. The fragrance of flowers, grass, and citrus mingled to form the most pleasant aroma. Insects chirped and birds called from the treetops. A butterfly floated lazily past me. I almost didn't notice it until the light caught its wings and they changed color from a deep plum, to teal, to peacock blue and back again. I stared as it fluttered to a cluster of hydrangeas of the softest pink. It rested there until the flowers began to rustle. The butterfly flew off, and a small, white rabbit hopped into view.

The rabbit's fluffy chalk-colored fir was in stark contrast

to the pink rim around its red eyes. Something about that bothered me, but when I tried to pin it down I realized it wasn't just the bunny that was giving me a weird feeling; there was something else, and I couldn't quite put my finger on it. The answer was about to come to me when Becca interrupted my thought process.

"We're outside," she announced flatly.

George blinked a few times before answering. "Well, yes."

"The word 'sanctum' is usually used in reference to someplace *indoors*. Why are we out here, and why would this matter so much to Kaly?" She waved her hand with ruby-red painted nails at me. Leave it to Becca to pack nail polish while she was getting ready to flee for her life.

Somewhere a dog howled a long two-toned cry. Soon it was joined by other, similar calls. It was the chattering, screeching, and grunts that came afterwards that finally jarred an explanation loose in my brain.

"The animals," I blurted.

Both of them turned to look at me.

"That's what's so weird; I knew something felt off. It's the animals. You have animals here that don't usually appear in the wild, like that albino rabbit and the iridescent butterfly. And the noises from the others; they don't usually live together. Those are beagles howling, right? And primates screeching, and are those… cows I hear?"

George was smiling, but Becca still looked confused.

"The Sanctum is where you keep the animals that Ross, um, *liberates*?" I asked without expecting an answer.

George responded anyway. "Yes! You're very observant. They are mostly from testing facilities, though we do have some pigs, goats, and sheep that Ross found along with the cows. They were in a horribly maintained petting zoo. And we have a separate area for the two tigers he rescued from cages in a millionaire's basement. Oh, and there is a small family of dolphins in our bay that Ross brought over from… well, it's probably best I don't tell you which government had them or why. Eventually we'd like to release them back into the wild. It looks very promising.

We also have some animals here that you won't see anywhere else in the world. Genetically modified or cross breeds we've discovered that were created by other, less-reputable scientists. We bring them here to safely live out their lives in as natural an environment as we can give them.

"I thought The Sanctum would be of interest to you since you're a veterinarian." He stuffed his hands into his lab coat pockets and then lifted his shoulders and eyebrows all at the same time. "I was also kind of hoping you might stick around for a while. We haven't had an animal doctor here for a long time. Our last doctor retired and we've had the worst luck finding a replacement. It'd be good to have them looked at if you wouldn't mind?"

"Who's been taking care of them up until now?" I asked.

"That would be Abe. I'll introduce you. He's the unofficial animal keeper right now. He'll be happy you're here. He's been begging for someone to take over The Sanctum. It doesn't leave him much time for research."

"What sort of research?"

"Mostly studies on marine animals. He was so excited when Ross brought the dolphins. Then he kinda got roped into helping with the other animals, too."

"This place is pretty amazing," I admitted. "How big are the enclosures?"

"We don't like to call them enclosures. Aside from the fence between the tigers and all the other animals, we don't have any barriers other than the natural ones, like the mountain or the ocean. The Sanctum itself is five miles long, three for most of the animals and another two for the tigers. It's almost a mile to the ocean from here, and it's at least that wide along all five miles."

I gave a low whistle. "Wow, that's a large enclo… um, I mean area." I ran a hand through my hair and tugged through a couple tangles. "How do you care for them all in an area this size?"

"We have feeding stations spread across The Sanctum. We chip all our animals with trackers and Abe keeps an eye on the food troughs and the trackers to ensure everyone is making it to the stations regularly."

"Best zoo ever," Becca said.

George frowned. "It's not a zoo. It's a sanctuary."

She held up her hands. "I was kidding, relax. It really is impressive though. I'd be glad to help out too if you'd like."

George nodded enthusiastically. "Abe will be happy to hear it!" Turning to me, he continued, "You may want to do an inventory before the supply run tomorrow. See if there's anything we need. Like I said, it's been a while since we've had an actual animal doctor here. We've been lucky thus far, but it would be good to make sure we are prepared. Abe does what he can but doesn't know much about what medical supplies to keep on hand. Did I mention that I'm glad you're here?"

He showed us the storage shed that was cleverly hidden behind some thickly growing cannas and tangy scented hibiscus shrubs. It was surprisingly large on the inside. There were four ATVs lined up against one wall. By the back wall were more bags of dog food and an industrial-sized walk-in freezer. I peeked inside the small freezer window and immediately wished I hadn't. There were four frozen deer hanging from large hooks in the ceiling.

George heard my startled cry and quickly explained when he saw what caused my alarm. "It's for the tigers. We have plant-based protein food for the other animals, but we just can't get the tigers to eat it. So we contracted some off-the-grid hunters to supply us with deer and the occasional wild boar. Once a month they airdrop a delivery out in the middle of the ocean and Tunui goes to pick it up. They use beacons or some such. It's such a convoluted process, but Ross worked it out. He loves that cloak-and-dagger stuff."

"I see." It was all I could think to say.

"I'm sure Abe can assist you with that part if it makes you nervous or uncomfortable," he said as though reading my mind.

There were a couple desks along the wall by the door. George slid open a drawer and pulled out a laptop. He handed it to me and then rustled through the desk again, this time pulling out a map. It was identical to the larger one that filled most of the wall behind the two desks.

"The computer is yours now. It has tracking software on it, so you can keep an eye on the animals. I'll show you how to use it if you want to boot it up."

"That's okay. Ross already showed me when we chipped the latest bunch of beagles. He mentioned there were other dogs on the island but failed to tell me how many, or that there were other animals here, too, for that matter," I said ruefully.

"We are all a bit too used to playing our hands close to the vest around here. Don't take it personally; it's become a habit if we talk to people we don't know well." George placed the map in my free hand. "You can keep this map with you when you're out in the field. At least until you familiarize yourself with the area."

"Thanks." I stuck the map in my pocket and cradled the large laptop in my arms.

"I'm sure you'll have lots of questions, so I also picked up two of these." He patted his pockets until he found what he was looking for. After pulling two wristbands out, he handed one to me and one to Becca. "You may have already discovered that your cell phones don't work here. Only these special, network-specific ones will work and only here on the island; unless you have an encryption key. All the numbers are pre-programmed into the phones, so if you have questions you can reach anyone on the island."

I set the computer down on the desk and examined the small device. "This is a cell phone?"

"Yes, it works like this." George flipped his hand over so his palm was facing up.

What I thought was his watch turned out to be identical to the wristband I now held in my hand. He pressed a button, and his arm lit up. I stared in amazement and realized it wasn't just a light, it was a projection. The small apparatus turned his forearm into what looked like a smartphone screen.

"Here you can make calls." He pointed at one of the icons. "You can also view files and data, but you have to set that up from a computer." He pointed to a couple other icons that were shining on his light-colored skin. "It can do much of what a smart phone does. Though access to the Web is limited, you can still get to some sites. And though you can install Candy Crush, I wouldn't. It's highly addictive."

He laughed at his own joke. Becca and I smiled politely at him.

"Thanks," I replied and then resumed my investigation of the new technology.

The wonders of the island seemed never-ending. I lost myself in the gadget's speed, accuracy, and the way the light interacted with my fingers.

"Kaly." Art's southern drawl crept from the small speaker on my new phone.

I screeched involuntarily before realizing what had just happened. "Art?" I leaned close to my communicator, uncertain where the mic was.

"Yes."

"How did you know how to find me?"

"I can hear any conversation that happens near an

electronic microphone that is connected to the network. George stated that he would be giving you a communication device. Two new devices came online, and I went with the one that picked up your voice the loudest. It was an educated guess."

"You can hear everything?" Becca looked at her new acquisition with less fascination than she had only moments ago.

"Yes," Art replied. "That is how I also know that Henry is looking for you but is uncertain where to find you."

"He's looking for me?" I cut in. "Where is he, is everything okay?"

"He is located in the place they call the examination room. I believe he needs your assistance with Mort."

I immediately forgot about my new toy and went straight for the door of the shed. "What's wrong? Is he hurt or sick?"

"It is uncertain. I believe that is why he requires your assistance."

I got to the area where we first entered The Sanctum and paused. Becca and George were right behind me. I whipped around, grabbed George by the shoulders, and shook him in a panic. "Where's the door? How do I get the door open?"

George broke free from my grasp and dug through vines at about eye level on the side of the mountain. He found what he was looking for and leaned his weight into his hand. A loud click sounded, followed by a rumbling noise. Two large doors opened, and I brushed past George to hurry inside.

Retracing our earlier path at a sprint, I made it back to

the exam room in no time. Unfortunately, I didn't get the door open fast enough and face planted into its unforgiving metal, my hand slipping off the handle. Growling, I rubbed my nose with one hand and used the other to try once again to open the door. The second attempt proved successful.

Henry glanced up from where Mort was lying on the exam table. An agitated rhesus monkey jumped from the second exam table, down to the floor, and then up onto Mort's table. I knew it was Lucky when she started making quick signs with her hands and then leaned over to hug Mort.

"What happened? Is he hurt?" I shouted.

"No, but I think he's sick. He's been restless and threw up, and, and then he had a seizure. I-I don't know what's wrong. I didn't know how to find you. Please help him!"

It was the pleading, urgent look in Henry's eyes that got me moving. I ransacked the drawers and cabinets looking for supplies, wishing I was back at my clinic, where I had everything I could possibly need and I knew exactly where it was. I located a stethoscope that was covered in a layer of dust. Not even bothering to clean them off, I shoved the eartips in my ears. His heart rate was elevated, and there was a slight tremor that ran through his body every so often. The pressure of the stethoscope and the familiar sounds coming through it put me in the zone. My body relaxed. My hands were steady. My voice grew even and calm.

"What did he eat?" I asked "It was probably something he ate."

Henry shook his head and shrugged, his demeanor

calming in response to my 'in-charge' attitude. "I'm not sure, just the normal food unless he got into something when I wasn't looking."

"Lucky!" Becca pointed to the monkey who was now climbing one of the storage cabinets. "She gave Mort food the other night. Maybe she gave him something."

"Ask her if she gave him something," I instructed.

Becca turned to Lucky. "Did you give him something to eat?"

I gave my nearly hysterical best friend a look. "Becks, she speaks sign language; you have to use signs."

"Right, right, sorry." She made a couple signs with her hands.

Lucky jumped to the floor so fast Becca squeaked and backed into a utensil tray.

"Calm down, it's okay," I stated assertively. "What's she saying? It's something with a C."

Lucky was making a C with one hand and circling it over the back of her other hand. She kept making it over and over until Becca made a nodding motion with her right fist.

"She's saying chocolate," Becca informed me, her eyes wide with fear. "That's bad right? Isn't chocolate toxic for dogs?"

"It can be," I replied. Making eye contact with Henry I continued. "You said he threw up?"

Henry nodded.

I matched his head bobbing with my own. "That's good; it's his body fighting off the toxicity. I need some things that I'm not finding here, but I'm sure they have them down in the infirmary. George, run down there and get me some benzodiazepine. Oh, and I need to do a urinalysis and to administer IV fluid, so I'll need—"

George cut me off. "Wait, I don't think I'll be able to remember all this."

Becca grabbed some paper and a pen out of one of the drawers I had left open. "Here, write it down."

I scribbled everything I needed and handed the pad to George. He glanced at it and then back up at me.

"I can't read this."

"You don't have to." I rolled my eyes and shoved him toward the door. "Yates used to work in an ER, she'll be able to read it. Now go!"

Art's voice was calm but it still startled me as it floated up from my wrist communicator. "I have informed Dr. Yates of the list of items you need. She is gathering them now."

"Oh, thanks Art," I said toward my wrist. "I keep forgetting he's there," I mumbled to no one in particular.

Lucky was jumping from one object to the next, chattering loudly. She would stop to make a sign over and over and then resume her sporadic leaping and climbing.

"What's she saying?" I asked Becca.

Becca watched Lucky until she made the sign again. Becca's eyes softened. "She keeps saying she's sorry."

"Tell her it's okay." I pressed my stethoscope up against Mort's rapidly rising and falling chest. "Why don't you take her and see if you can find Ross. I think she's just making Mort more anxious."

It took Becca and Henry both a few minutes to calm Lucky down. Then a few more minutes to convince her to leave with Becca to go find Ross. But once the two of them left, the room felt a lot more peaceful, and Mort's breathing seemed to slow a little too.

I let out a long breath and gave Henry a weak smile. "What a day, huh?"

Henry blinked a few times and tried unsuccessfully to return my smile. "I don't know how this happened. He's been with me all day. Lucky kept showing up wherever we went, but I honestly never even saw her give him anything." He was gripping the table so hard his knuckles were turning white.

"It's going to be all right." I softly rubbed his hands until they released their death grip. "I hear she's pretty sneaky. It was an accident. And I'm here now, and I'll do everything I can to make sure Mort recovers fully."

"Will he be okay?"

I chewed thoughtfully on my lip as I surveyed Mort's limp body. "I'll want to keep him under careful observation for the next eight to twelve hours, but he's a champ; I'm sure he'll pull through."

"I'll stay with you," he stated resolutely.

"Are you sure?"

He nodded.

"Maybe you could go grab us some coffee then; it's going to be a long night."

He finally smiled and was about to leave when Mort began to seize again. I held Mort's sides gently to make sure he wouldn't fall off the table. I quickly cleaned up the small puddle of urine left in the seizure's wake. Then tenderly stroked Mort and spoke reassuringly to him as his eyes darted wildly around in pain and fear.

"I've got him," I said, when I saw the same look swirl in Henry's eyes. His panic was rising, and I knew he needed a distraction. "Go and find George. Tell him to get back here with my benzodiazepine!"

He hesitated like he wanted to say something, but then he spun on his heel and raced out the door.

Mort whimpered softly.

"Hang in there, buddy," I murmured. "Henry still needs you, and so do I. So you gotta stick around for a while, okay?"

He looked up at me with his brown, soulful eyes, and I blinked back tears as I prayed that we would both make it through the next eight hours.

Chapter 7

The night stretched out as I monitored Mort's vital signs. The benzodiazepine helped with the seizures, and his heart rate evened out. The urinalysis didn't show any sign of organ failure, which helped me relax a little. I dozed a few times in the chair next to where Mort slept, my head leaning on the exam table. I woke up to Mort whimpering but realized he wasn't awake. Gently petting his head and rubbing his ears, I whispered soothing words to him until he stopped crying and fell back into a more restful sleep.

Henry was curled on top of the other exam table, a roll of paper towels cradling his head. I watched him as he slept, letting my eyes move from his thick, brown hair to his somewhat-pointed nose, over to his chiseled cheeks and down to his subtly dimpled chin. My eyes lingered on his full lips, and all I could think about was what it might be like to kiss them; they looked so soft. And then I felt guilty for thinking about that while Mort was like this so got up to check his vitals for the umpteenth time. My legs protested the movement after sitting for so long.

His pulse was steady, so I took a moment to retrieve the

bottle of painkillers that Henry so graciously brought from my room. The rattling of the pills woke Henry. He groaned and rubbed his neck as he slowly sat up. He swung his legs over the side of the table and let them dangle. I smiled at how young the action made him seem, especially as he worried about his sick best friend. My new wrist phone and my stomach both told me it was time for breakfast.

"He's doing a lot better." I picked the stethoscope up from the table and slung it around my neck. "He's through the worst of it and should be in the clear now."

Henry's sigh of relief could not have been any bigger. He hopped down from his table and was at Mort's side in two long strides. "Did you hear that, buddy? You're going to be okay." He tenderly rubbed his bulldog's belly.

I pulled up the contact list on my phone and was pleased to find Becca's new number programed into it. Tapping two places on my arm was all it took, and soon she was on the line.

"Hey," she said, mumbling around what I assumed to be food.

"Morning," I laughed. "I take it you're up at breakfast?"

"Mm hmm."

"Don't suppose you'd mind bringing some down for us workin' folk?"

"Yeah, giv' me a minute to finish 'n I'll bring you somfin'," she said around another bite of food.

My arm started to flash, or rather light from my phone pulsed across my forearm. Incoming call. I frowned. "It looks like Ross is calling me."

"K," she responded, and then I could tell she'd hung up.

Henry looked at me with a bit of a frown. I shrugged and tapped my finger where my skin glowed with the words "accept incoming call from Ross."

"Good morning, love; I hope it's not too early." Ross' voice came through loud and clear and more sultry than I was prepared for.

"Uh, hi Ross." I fidgeted with the wristband, flicked my fingers through the light beams, and vowed to learn how to control the volume as soon as humanly possible. "What's up?"

I could hear the grin in his voice, as though he could read my awkward thoughts through the high-tech phone. "I was just calling to check on your dog; is he all right?" He slathered the concern thickly over his words.

"Yeah, he seems to be doing a lot better now."

"Good. You know Lucky feels truly awful."

"It was an accident, but I don't suppose you can explain that to a monkey."

Ross laughed. "Well, I keep telling her it's okay, but I think she won't calm down until she sees that he's better. Any chance we could pop by?"

"You should wait a while before you bring her." I glanced at Mort. "He's still not back to his old self yet. He needs his rest, and I'm worried Lucky will get him worked up. She seems to have that effect."

"I get it. Think you'll still be able to help introduce the new beagles with me this morning?"

I stared at my wristband, my mouth fell open a little.

"Hello? Kaly, are you still there?"

I cleared my throat. "Yes, sorry. I forgot about that. I don't think I'll be able to now. Do you have anyone else that can help?"

"Of course, no worries. You just get your dog back to feeling his best. I'll round up some others to fill in for you."

As soon as the call ended, Henry gripped my hand. "How long do you think it'll be until he's... ready for a visit from Lucky?"

"Not much longer." I squeezed his hand. "He's still young; I think he'll recover quickly and fully."

Henry's shoulders slumped. "We're supposed to go on that supply run today."

"That's right! I'm supposed to make a list of things I need." I reluctantly released myself from Henry's grasp and started rummaging through drawers. After finding the pen and paper from the night before, I began to jot down the things every decent veterinarian clinic should have. Noticing Henry's worried expression, I stopped. "What's wrong?"

He stared down at Mort, who was beginning to wake up. "I can't just leave him while we go *shopping,* can I?"

"Oh," I joined him at Mort's table and pulled the stethoscope from around my neck. "I guess I can write down what I need and stay here with him." I listened to Mort's heart beat, nice and steady.

"Maybe we could find someone else to keep an eye on him?" Henry suggested.

"I'm sure Ross would."

Henry grunted and then coughed as though to cover it

up. "George mentioned someone who takes care of the animals in The Sanctuary. What about him?"

"I think his name is Abe."

Mort wiggled and worked to stand up. He was a little shaky on his feet. Henry looked at me and I nodded, so he picked Mort up from the table and gently placed him on the floor. The dog's collar jingled as he purposely shook his whole body, as though to rid himself of the cobwebs of illness and drugs. Then he started sniffing around the room, exploring the new and unfamiliar scents. He circled so quickly I didn't have time to process what was happening. He began his business before I even had the chance to look for paper or puppy pads.

"Mortimer!" Henry cried out when Mort was mid-business.

"It's okay." I laughed. "It's a good sign. It means his kidney function is okay."

Henry's smile made the room ten times brighter. "I'll get some paper towels and clean this up."

"Am I interrupting anything?" Becca quipped from the doorway, hands once again full of a tray of food.

Henry began laughing. "Sorry, sorry," he said through gasps. He waved his hands and seemed to try to stop but was unsuccessful. Tears soon filled his eyes and he tried to suck in breaths between wheezes of laughter.

"I think he's just tired and relieved," I explained when Becca gave me a confused look. "It's been a long night."

We ate our breakfast in a tired silence after Henry was finally able to compose himself. It was a simple hash recipe with crisply sautéed sweet potatoes and golden russet potatoes. The garlic and caramelized onion melded together to add just the right savory flavor. I couldn't suppress my satisfied groan and was reluctant to drink my water; I didn't want to wash away the taste.

After we finished eating, Henry took Mort for a walk and to see if he could find Abe. One call to George let us know that the supply run couldn't be pushed a day, so Henry was going to see if Abe would watch Mort. I finished my list for the run while Becca took the dishes back up to the mess hall. I met her back in our common room, and we discussed what personal supplies we would need from our little shopping trip.

Gaël soon came by to take us to the boat dock. He and Becca exchanged shy smiles and sideways glances along the way. I picked at my clothes and played with my wristband, trying, unsuccessfully, not to catch these private moments. I tried to think of something to say that could end the awkward silence, but nothing came to mind. So we continued our trek, and I pretended not to notice their quiet flirtations.

The boat was docked in a large cavern. The sun hit the water and bounced around to produce shimmering waves of light across the walls and ceiling. A decent-sized boat was moored along the sturdy dock, its sails tucked away neatly, awaiting their chance to once again capture the salty winds. It rocked leisurely, as small waves lapped against its sides.

Henry was already on the boat, loading crates and bundles of various sizes. George shouted something to Tunui from the dock. I watched Tunui in fascination. The weathered gentleman we'd met when we first arrived on the island maneuvered around the vessel like he had every nook and cranny memorized. I'd never seen someone get a boat ready to go, but I guessed it looked a lot like what I was watching.

I followed Gaël and Becca down the dock and onto the boat. Its lazy rocking felt a lot less tame now that I was subject to it. My stomach rolled a little in protest, as though contemplating whether to clear out my breakfast. I took some deep breaths and tried to convince my insides not to revolt. Tunui appeared like a phantom at my side.

"Here," he said, in his thick accent. "Chew this; it will help."

And just as quickly, he disappeared again.

I sniffed the small, gnarled root and realized it was ginger. Hesitantly I popped it in my mouth. Flavor burst across my tongue with the first bite. It took all my willpower not to spit it out; the sharp tang was overwhelming. But we weren't even out of the cave when I noticed the calming effect it had on my stomach. We slipped quietly out into open water. The sound of the surf grew louder and the air grew warmer when we hit the sunshine.

Glancing behind me, I realized there were long strands of ivy being held back by ropes, like curtains framing a window. The ropes loosened, and the ivy lowered slowly after our exit; soon the cave disappeared behind them, as though it never existed.

"Everything is so cleverly hidden," I mentioned to Henry.

"How do you think they've managed to keep this place a secret so long?" He smirked, and I couldn't tear my eyes away from his lips.

That is until he started working the rigging. His muscles were taut under his fitted t-shirt, and I'm embarrassed to admit how long I stared. Even the unfurling of the sails weren't enough to draw my attention away. Only when Becca rammed her shoulder into mine did I break my stupor.

"I've always wanted to go sailing." She sighed.

"And to think it only took being chased by a ruthless multi-billion-dollar corporation and running for our lives to make that happen," I deadpanned.

"We should have discovered alien technology years ago." She matched my tone.

I couldn't hold a straight face any longer, and soon Becca was laughing as hard as I was. We continued to ride the waves in a happy silence, letting the wind fill our hair the way it filled the sails.

Gaël offered some sailing lessons along the way, pointing out and naming the different parts of the boat. He showed us a few tricks to trim the sails and how to tie basic knots. I was keenly interested in learning about sailing, but Becca was more preoccupied with learning about Gaël. After a while, I left them alone and joined Henry at the back of the boat, where he was holding our course steady with a large, intricately carved wheel.

"Wanna give it a try?" He smiled at me with one eyebrow raised.

I grinned back. "Sure!"

He pulled me over, so I was between him and the helm. Gently, he took both of my hands, placing them on two spindles of the outer circle of the wheel. His arms framed me there, strong and safe. A warm buzz tingled down my spine. I felt his breath on my neck. My knees weakened, and I leaned into him. His soft murmur did nothing to strengthen my stance, and I melted into him as he spoke.

"I used to go sailing a lot with my dad when I was younger."

I smiled at the thought of him as a child, sailing the world with his father.

"After my mom left us, it was the only thing that seemed to keep him tethered."

Turning slightly, I frowned up at him.

His warm smile released the tension of my downturned lips. "It was honestly some of the greatest experiences of my life, sailing with my dad. I don't think we would have had that if she'd stayed. So I'm no longer upset with her for leaving. I remember the good times he and I had instead, on oceans just like this."

We both turned to watch the sea glitter and froth ahead of us.

"You don't sail with him anymore?" I asked.

I could feel him shake his head, his chin grazing the my hair slightly with each back and forth motion. "He passed away a couple weeks before I turned sixteen…. Cancer." The word was soft and sad; more acceptance than anger.

"I'm sorry," I replied meekly.

He took a deep breath and let it out slowly before

continuing. "Actually, that's why I became a scientist. I want to discover the cure so no other child has to lose a parent that way."

"If anyone can do it, it's you and your island of scientists," I murmured.

His arms squeezed tighter around me, and I nestled into him.

"That's what makes this discovery of alien life so exciting," he whispered. "Their technology is obviously more advanced than ours, so maybe their medicine is too. If we can meet them and exchange knowledge with them…. Can you imagine a world without cancer?"

"I can now," I said softly.

Becca's loud gasp brought us out of our safe, intimate cocoon.

"Look!" She pointed.

I broke out of Henry's arms and rushed to Becca's side.

"Whales! I can't believe I'm finally seeing real ones in the wild!" Becca sounded like a schoolgirl with a crush.

"You scared me," I scolded her. "I thought it was more pirates or something."

"Calm down there, Jack Sparrow." She rolled her eyes. "I wonder what kind they are."

Gaël came up next to her and squinted at the pod as they breached the ocean's surface. "They're Cuvier's beaked whales."

Becca gaped at him.

He shrugged. "I've spent a lot of time with Abe; he studies them. He's hacked into the tracker system the scientists from Mo'orea use, so he knows when the groups are close to the island."

"So cool," Becca breathed, turning back to stare at the surfacing behemoths.

One of the more curious mammals swam next to our boat. I grabbed the metal wire railing and leaned out to get a better look. It was almost close enough to touch, and I reached out my hand just as a large wave tossed our boat. My stomach flipped as my body soared up over the railing. The cold blast of water was a shock, and I inadvertently opened my mouth, taking in a huge gulp of saltwater.

Under the waves, I heard the muffled sound of shouting, and something splashed in the water beside me. Fighting the panic, I struggled to break the surface and tried to forget about the large, unpredictable creature nearby. A blurry blob grabbed me as I finally managed to get my head above water. I thrashed against my unknown attacker, fearing that perhaps the aquatic beast thought I was prey or a toy to investigate.

"It's me. Kaly, it's me!" Henry shouted over and over until I was finally able to comprehend his words.

I stopped flailing as Henry's powerful arm came from behind me and wrapped around my waist. I leaned back into him and helped kick when I realized he was attempting to swim back toward the boat.

Two more hands reached down from above and helped pull me out of the water. A waterlogged Henry hefted himself up after me.

Gaël held my shoulders and looked into my eyes. "Are you all right?"

I coughed and coughed, trying to clear away the saltwater. I nodded. "Where's Becca?" I asked, looking around in growing alarm.

Gaël jerked his head toward the back of the boat. "She's holding the helm to make sure the boat didn't veer away from you."

He pulled me to my feet. Becca's face filled with relief when she caught sight of us. I gave her a shaky wave. She waved too and then quickly placed her hand back on the wooden wheel, taking her job seriously.

Henry was wringing out his shirt when I threw my arms around him. "You saved me." I could feel his heart pounding as I held onto him.

"Always," he whispered into my ear, his voice husky. He pulled back to look me in the eye, his gaze heavy. "You sure you're okay?"

I nodded, looking up at him as ocean water dripped from my lashes.

He brushed away a strand of hair that was plastered to my face. Then, gently tipping my chin up toward him, he leaned down slowly.

"Land, ho!" Becca shouted, effectively breaking the moment.

Henry and I abruptly pulled away from each other.

"Really?" Henry looked thwarted and amused at the same time.

I couldn't help but laugh.

"Well, she's not wrong," Gaël chuckled, pointing at an island that was growing larger by the moment.

Henry's sigh was overly dramatic. "I think there are some towels down below. Do you want to see if you can find them while we prep the boat for docking?"

I gave him an apologetic smile. "Sure."

Below deck, I rummaged through the cabinets in search of something to dry off with. There were cabinets full of food, dishes, and first aid supplies. Tools, linens, and what I was looking for were in the next place I searched. I pulled out a stack of towels, and a handgun fell to the floor with a dull thud. A quick look around told me I was still alone. I shoved it back under the linens and closed the door. Guns made me nervous, especially after my recent run-ins with Pastern's men. It seemed out of place on Nowhere Island or even on one of their boats. Making a mental note to ask about the firepower, in my distracted state, I went the wrong way and ended up in the engine room.

The boat slowed, causing me to fall forward a few steps; Gaël and Henry must have taken in the sails. I covered my ears as the engine kicked in. Its aggressive, harsh churning filled the small room from inside a large metal cage. The smell of diesel drove me back the way I'd come and up to the fresh ocean air on the boat's deck.

I handed Henry a couple of the towels and used one to dry my own clothes and hair. Gaël expertly guided our boat past a large bay with cruise ships and other vessels coming and going. Just beyond the large bay was a smaller inlet that we slipped through. To one side was a resort with cute bungalows lining the turquoise waters. Various buildings and private docks dotted the rest of the coast.

The boat slowed, and Gaël turned the wheel as we closed in on one of the long wooden piers. We softly jostled against the rubber bumpers. Henry gracefully jumped ashore holding an oversized rope and with a quick flourish tied off the boat. He helped me up beside him while Gaël tied off the other end and then helped Becca onto the jetty.

"This is Mo'orea!" Henry waved an arm toward the low-lying buildings, nestled in the valley of tall, forested hills. "Who's ready to do some shopping?"

Chapter 8

"Is it weird that no one is here to greet us?" Becca asked.

Gaël shook his head. "This dock is owned by the research facility. The locals are used to boats coming and going here. No one thinks twice about it. And the scientists who use it usually arrange their own transportation." He led the way up the dock and onto a dirt path.

There was a group of bicycles chained up and partially hidden under a copse of nearby trees. He pulled a ring of keys out of his pocket and started fitting them one at a time into the padlock. The fourth key was a perfect fit, and the lock clicked open. He unthreaded the chain and freed four of the bikes. The rest of the bikes he re-secured with the padlock. From another pocket, he pulled out a folded piece of paper. A quick glance was apparently all he needed, and then he silently took off on his bike, not waiting to make sure we were following.

The warm air, singing birds, and shining sun made me forget why I was here on this tropical island. It suddenly felt like a vacation, and I tipped my head back a little to take in the scenery and the heavenly scents coming from every direction. We followed him down a busy, paved road but soon turned onto a quieter side street made of dirt. The dust followed us all the way to what Gaël called a mall, but it was more of an outdoor marketplace. It had a remote, off-the-grid feel to it, but the selection was surprisingly extensive.

Gaël found a sympathetic shop owner and placed a call, while Becca, Henry, and I searched through the clothing racks for items that would fit us. After Gaël finished his call, we shopped the rest of the marketplace, picking up everything from our various lists. We ended our trip at a small eatery serving a delicious salad with fresh, vine-ripe tomatoes, creamy avocados, edible flowers, and lightly toasted nuts topped with a mango, honey, and pear dressing.

"I have someone from the research station meeting me here. He has the last of the items from my list. Then we can head back," Gaël said as he put down his fork and pushed his empty plate away.

"No rush." Becca smiled. "It's so beautiful here, we can stay as long as you want."

We talked and laughed, enjoying the location and the company. We ordered refill after refill of the strawberry lemonade, and Henry promised a nice tip to make our lengthy stay worthwhile to the proprietor. It was nearly another hour before Gaël's contact showed up in a rusty, mud-splattered Jeep. He went to talk with the car's owner, and after some discussion and hand waving, Gaël rejoined us and the man in the Jeep drove off.

"He's going to meet us at the dock," Gaël informed us.

"There's no way I'd be able to carry all that equipment on my bike."

"Shall we go?" Henry asked.

We nodded. Henry paid the tab, and we situated our bags on the luggage racks and handle bars of our bikes for our trip back to the boat. It was slow going with our new purchases balanced precariously on our well-worn bicycles. But eventually we made it back. The man from the jeep was already loading boxes onto our boat.

Becca, Gaël, and I transferred the rest of our purchases onboard while Henry locked up the bikes. Gaël shook hands with his contact, who took off in his jeep as Henry walked back up the path toward us.

He and Gaël untied our vessel from the pier and shoved us away from the shore.

"Gaël, can you get us underway?" Henry asked. "There's something I need to do."

Gaël nodded. After taking his place by the helm, he fired up the engines, and we were motoring our way out of the bay when Henry came back up from below. He had a small, black device in his hand that beeped and squawked intermittently. He put a finger to his lips before I could ask him about it. Gaël frowned and tilted his head but didn't say anything.

After being gone for a while, Henry came back with his fist closed around something. He nodded in the direction of a nearby sailboat. Gaël seemed to understand his unspoken request and immediately turned toward it. We soon overtook the smaller vessel, and Henry discreetly tossed whatever was in his hand. It bounced once and then settled in a pile of rope on the other boat's deck.

"We good?" Gaël asked.

"Yeah, that was the only one."

"What's happening?" Becca wondered.

"Someone put a tracker on our boat. Not sure if it had audio capabilities or not." Henry said.

Gaël steered our craft off in a new direction. "What made you think to look?"

"I thought I saw someone following your guy in the Jeep," Henry explained. "The same car was driving away when we rode up. Better safe than sorry, and looks like I was right. We better take the indirect route home to make sure they don't follow us the old-fashioned way."

Gaël blew out a breath and kept his head on a swivel as we glided out of the bay and into open water.

"What do we do if they follow us *the old-fashioned way*?" I frowned.

"We lead them off in the wrong direction," Henry smiled mischievously. "And then we incapacitate their craft."

I raised an eyebrow "Incapacitate?"

"We've got company," Gaël called out from the helm.

We followed his line of sight, and sure enough there was a speed boat holding a steady pace, barely visible behind us.

Henry sighed. "I guess the old bait and switch with the tracker didn't throw them off."

"Gotta get them closer for the EMP cannon to work," Gaël announced.

"Cannon?" Becca wrung her hands.

"Speed up, and when they pick up speed to keep up with us, cut the engines. They'll get close enough before they realize we've stopped," Henry instructed.

Gaël pushed the throttle all the way forward. The engine's steady thrum grew louder, and the vibrations intensified under my feet. Henry went below deck once again and came back up with what looked like an oversized radar gun.

"Have you used one of those before?" Gaël asked.

Henry nodded. After snapping the scope open, he flipped a couple switches and leaned the cannon against the railing post for support. Once aimed at the trailing boat, he called out, "Now!"

Gaël threw back the throttle and the boat slowed to a stop. Henry kept his eyes on the scope. The boat grew larger, and Henry waited until the lights on the side went from red to green, then pulled the trigger. The cannon gave off a loud pop like a large paperback book being dropped on a vinyl floor.

"Go, go, go!" Henry yelled, and Gaël gunned it once more.

The other boat fell farther and farther behind. We watched until it was out of sight, only then did Gaël alter our course to begin our journey back toward *Île de Nulle Part*.

"You just happen to have an EMP *cannon* around?" I directed my question at Henry's back since he was still keeping an eye out for other pursuing vessels.

"We can't risk being followed to the island," he said without turning around. "There are a number of precautions in place to make sure that doesn't happen. This is just one of them."

"How did they even know to tag our boat?" Gaël asked.

Henry finally turned around, letting the device hang by his side. "My guess would be they've bought someone off at the facility on Mo'orea. We're going to have to figure something else out for future supply runs."

Henry's shoulders slumped, and he set the cannon down on the roof of the boat's cabin. He ran a hand through his short, brown hair, leaving it sticking up in places. The setting sun caused him to squint as he turned to check for any further signs of pursuit. "Jacob is going to blame me."

"You mean he's going to blame *me*," I added.

Henry smiled sadly, meeting my eye. He shrugged.

"There's no way he could blame you," Gaël interjected. "We've been going to Mo'orea for a while now. It was only a matter of time before someone found us there. And now that Pastern is after that alien tech, it's not surprising they stepped up their game and found us."

"I'm sure he'll find some way for this to still be my fault." My laugh was humorless.

"Speaking of alien tech," Becca cut in. "What exactly are you going to do with it, other than play keep away with Pastern?"

Gaël looked at Henry, who shrugged and then nodded.

"We're getting things ready for their first visit." Gaël's eyes flicked from the waters ahead, over to Becca, and then back again. Checking his compass, he adjusted the wheel slightly and kept his eyes on the horizon.

"Their what now?" I sputtered.

For the first time since leaving the island, Henry looked excited. He started bouncing a little on his heels and waved his arms animatedly as he spoke. "They're coming, Kaly! They want to make contact. It's going to be the biggest event since, since, well, I don't even know when. And we get to be a part of it!"

"That's why I needed some special equipment from the research lab on Mo'orea," Gaël added. "I'm helping Art build a translator and a homing satellite to guide them here."

I grabbed onto the smaller mast by the helm to keep from falling over. The sea tossed the boat and my stomach as I tried to think through this new information.

Henry grabbed the EMP cannon and took it back down to the cabin. Becca grasped the same mast I clung to, and for a few moments we let the ocean lift and drop us in silence. When Henry returned, I had my questions all lined up like little soldiers.

"So when they come, where will the meeting take place?"

He took over steering the ship so Gaël could work the rigging and raise the sails. "There's an abandoned oil rig we have in mind. George and Tunui are going to go inspect it before our final decision."

"And who all will be in attendance for this auspicious visit?"

"Looking for an invitation?" He grinned slyly at me.

I tried to keep from smiling, but his steady gaze made it impossible. "I'm serious, Henry." I did my best to tame my face. "This is obviously a huge deal. Like leaders of the world kind of deal. So I can't help but wonder who all will make the list."

Henry grew serious. "I've spoken with our governing body on *Île de Nulle Part* and with Art to hear his thoughts on the matter. We all came to the agreement that it would just be the scientists on the island for now. Once we establish a relationship and communication, we can discuss with them how best to break the news to the world."

"You're making these decisions for everyone?"

"We thought about voting American Idol style, but the logistics of it were a bit of a nightmare, so we decided to go with this way instead." Henry once again cracked a smile.

I crossed my arms but had to quickly uncross them so I could grab the mast as a wave rocked the boat. "Don't be glib. You're really comfortable making this decision so unilaterally?"

"Our research facility has been making decisions like this for a long time. We have some of the top minds in the world here. We make life-or-death decisions every day. We don't take it lightly. Every precaution is in place to ensure both the highest safety and the best results. Sometimes it's best that we keep the circle small…. At first anyways. Something this large needs to be consumed in small bites. Any larger and then the politicians get involved, and there's no telling what can happen from that point."

I thought about it for a long time. Looking at Becca only earned me a shrug.

Finally, I spoke. "If the first meeting goes well, then you expand the circle? Bring other people in too, people like the government?"

"If it's agreeable to our guests."

"What if our *guests* aren't the altruistic sort? I've seen *Independence Day*."

He laughed, and it was just as magical as the first time I heard it. "You and your movie references. You seem to be hitting all the good ones."

"Yes, I'm fluent in movie quotes." I grinned.

A voice floated up from my wristband. "Is that a dialect worth translating? I am not finding such a language in any database."

I gasped. "Art! Do you eavesdrop on everyone's conversations or just mine?"

There was a pause and then Art responded. "I do not actively monitor all communications; however, there are parameters in my subroutines that make me aware of conversations that may involve me or my creators, so I might monitor those for pertinent information."

"And we were discussing the arrival of your creators," Henry added, like it all made sense.

"Yes," Art agreed. "And then you mentioned being fluent in a language I am unfamiliar with, and my programing prompted me to inquire about it."

Becca snorted. "It's not an actual language. It's a figure of speech."

"Like when Ross called you a cheeky monkey?" Art asked.

Her face reddened, and she glared at me. I caught Henry's eye and stifled a laugh.

"Yes," she said through clenched teeth.

I moved the conversation along to help her out. "Going back to the conversation that brought you to us Art, what do you think about the plan?"

"I agree with what the governing board has decided. I closely followed their discussion and contributed what I could with what I know about how my creators operate."

A thought suddenly occurred to me. "Why not meet on the island?"

Gaël answered, "We thought about that, but with how extensively space is monitored, we run the risk of someone noticing our visitors. So we need to meet somewhere else to make sure the island remains hidden, in case someone tracks their arrival."

Becca groaned and we all turned to look at her. "I'm sorry. It's not you, it's me. I think all this sun and surf is getting to me. Is there a bed on this thing? I'd like to lay down for a bit."

"I'll show you," Gaël offered.

After they were gone, Henry tipped his head and appraised me thoughtfully. "How are you feeling? Any sea or sun sickness?"

"I'm good."

"How about with the plan?"

I took a deep breath and let it out slowly. "I can see the merits of it."

"But you still have reservations?"

I bit my lip as I worked on forming my response. "I guess I was thinking that if it was announced to everyone, then Becca and I might be able to go home. But if we are still keeping it a secret, then we'll have to remain here."

"Are you completely devastated by the prospect of staying with me here for a while longer?" His tone was playful, but I could have sworn a bit of worry tinted his voice.

I looked away and kept my lips turned down for as long as I could, but they soon betrayed me and slipped upward. "I think I can manage spending more time with you."

His expression seemed to hold relief. "Good, because we still haven't gone on our date yet. I hope you didn't forget. I certainly haven't."

I felt my cheeks heat up. "Sorry, I had to postpone it. I was saving your dog's life as I recall."

"For which I am extremely grateful." He moved a little closer. "And I will show you *how* grateful when you join me for dinner, say, when we get back to the island?"

"It's a date." I gently touched his arm. My stomach flipped with the contact and not from the ocean this time. "I better go check on Becca."

He smiled his million-kilowatt smile, and I pretended it was a wave that made my knees give out on me. I held onto the boat railing until I made it to the stairs. I could still feel his eyes on me until I climbed below deck in search of my queasy best friend.

Tunui was waiting for us on the island's hidden dock. He secured the ropes and then offered his hand to help Becca and then me onto the jetty.

"I need to speak with George," Henry announced. "Then

I'd like to clean up a bit before our dinner."

Becca smiled wickedly and nudged me hard in the ribs.

"Shut up," I hissed at her.

"I didn't say anything." She gave me her most innocent look.

If Henry noticed our exchange, he didn't acknowledge it. "Kaly, I'll come get you in about an hour if that's okay?"

"See you then," I squeaked.

Gaël handed us all the bags we had acquired from our shopping excursion, and I used mine as a bulldozer to shove Becca off in front of me. We made it back to our suite without uttering a single word. Every time she started to say something, I would shush her. Once back in our common room, she finally broke through my wall of silence.

"You're going on a date with your booooyfriend," she said in a sing–song tone.

"How old are you, twelve?"

"Look who's talking. You're the one who can't even discuss it without turning red."

"Shut up and help me figure out what I'm going to wear."

She put her hands on her hips and smirked. "And you almost didn't get that cute new dress today. This is why you always need to listen to me. I know what's best for you."

My eyes rolled instinctively. "So you've told me a thousand times."

She then did something only a BFF would do—she sniffed me. Crinkling her nose, she shoved me toward my room. "Go shower first. You smell like Red's Best."

"Whatever would I do without you?" I asked straight-faced.

"Go on your last first date smelling like a fish market?"

I stopped and whirled around to face her. "My *last* first date?"

"Let's just say I have a good feeling about this one." She winked and gave me one final push into my room. Before I could respond, she closed the door in my face.

Chapter 9

Not even in my wildest dreams could I have planned a better first date. A table was set up on the beach, complete with an intricate lace tablecloth. High-gloss, white porcelain plates, rimmed with delicate patterns in silver, were set out with matching utensils. The elaborate, chrome candlesticks glowed softly and dripped with crystals more than wax. Glass domes covered trays of fragrant, colorful food waiting to be devoured. Henry pulled out my chair and helped me arrange a napkin in my lap.

The sun was setting behind the dormant volcano and poured its final colors into the sky with splashes of reds and oranges that bled into the various hues of blue. Rose petals were sprinkled along a path that led from the table to a small row boat nearby, its oars tucked neatly by its sides. Hidden speakers played soft classical music that mixed evenly with the gentle sounds of the waves washing up on the shore of the large bay.

"You mentioned not being a big drinker." Henry pulled a bottle of sparkling cider from the ice bucket next to him and poured us both a glassful of the amber liquid. "So I got this instead."

"It's perfect," I gushed, taking my glass with a shaky hand.

"I never knew I was living life in black and white," he said, his glass raised in the air. "Until you came along and showed me the beauty and richness of a life lived full of color."

I blinked back tears and ran through a bunch of replies in my head before settling on simply speaking the truth. "I always promised myself I would never allow a man to change me. But I realize now that when you meet the right person, you kinda change each other. And it's not a bad thing, if the change means you're growing closer."

He clinked my glass without breaking our intense eye contact. "To growing closer."

I took a shaky sip and set my glass down before I could drop it. We ate and talked and laughed well past sunset. The sky was clear as the moon and stars made their nightly appearance. The conversation came as easily as it did our first night on the island. And whenever our hands touched, I had to catch my breath. Each time felt like both the first and as though we had held hands for countless lifetimes.

When the darkness had fully settled around us, Henry stood and helped me out of my chair. I felt giddiness mingled with disbelief; the date was so perfect I was worried it was all just a dream and I would wake up at any second.

"I have one more surprise for you," Henry announced. "That is, if you aren't too tired?"

My heart played the rhythm it had invented just for Henry. "I'm not too tired."

He took my hand and led me down the flower-strewn pathway. Once I was seated inside, he carefully moved the boat off the sand and climbed in himself. I waited for him to start rowing, but he merely sat there, looking at me with a roguish smile on his lips.

I willed my face not to turn red under his stare. "What?"

"Do you trust me?"

"I don't think I'd be on this island if I didn't," I quipped.

He pulled out a jade-colored silk scarf and leaned forward, a questioning look in his eyes. I peeked at the scarf and then back up at him. His face was so full of boyish innocence, all I could do was bite my lower lip and nod.

Gently, he tied the smooth material around my eyes and then began to row. The sound of crickets slowly faded. I was about to ask him how much longer, when the oars stopped splashing and the boat slowed its forward motion. My nerves started to prick as we sat there rocking gently in the calm bay.

"Ready?" Henry finally asked.

"I think so," I whispered.

He pulled the blindfold off and grinned at me. I blinked a few times and looked around. We were in the middle of the bay, but I wasn't sure what I was supposed to be looking at, so I turned my attention back to Henry.

"I don't understand, what's the surprise?"

His laugh skipped across the waters like a smooth, flat stone. He grabbed one of the oars. "Watch this."

It was like a real-life magic trick. He dipped the oar into the water and it blazed to life. Like the oar was a comet, and it flashed a trail of light through the darkened waters. I gasped and stared in awe as he continued to light up the ocean with the oar. Everywhere the paddle went, the water glowed a hauntingly bright blue.

"How?" was all I could coax out.

"Bioluminescent algae," he explained. "Abe brought it over from Malta to study. I glows when its agitated. See?" He dipped his hand into the waters and the glowing burst all around his fingers.

I followed his lead and stuck my hand in the water. My mouth dropped open, but I didn't care; I only had eyes for the brilliant glow of the spectacular water. Dipping my arm in up to my elbow, my skin glowed the mysterious blue. Even after pulling my hand out, the algae glowed for a few seconds along my entire arm.

Henry's smile went from wonderment to mischievous, and before I could say another word, he jumped out of the boat. The water exploded brightly around him as if he were a bomb detonating. He surfaced, covered in a fading blanket of sapphire light. I didn't give it a second thought before jumping in after him, marveling at the incandescence of my body with every movement. We splashed and laughed like two children making the discovery of a lifetime. The night seemed made for magic, and we were made to bear witness.

My body grew tired long before my wonder did. Henry and I clung to the side of the boat so we could float a little longer in the enchanting sea. He took in a mouthful of water and spat it at me. I stopped mid-laugh, captivated by the glowing of his lips. Emboldened by the bewitching events of the evening, I leaned forward and kissed him, long and slow. We let go of the boat and slowly sank under the luminous waves. This time I felt like we were the ones causing the water to light up.

When my lungs were about to burst, I led our entwined bodies to the surface. Henry pulled himself into the boat and then reached down to help me. His muscular arms made the motion seem effortless, as he lifted me up and over the side. We sat for a few moments to catch our breath, water dripping from our hair and clothes.

"Tonight was perfect," I murmured, afraid to break the evening's spell.

"You're perfect." His tone matched mine.

I couldn't hold his heavy stare. My fingers twirled nervously in the hem of my clingy dress, watching the lights twinkle and fade. Nothing clever came to mind, so I just whispered, "Thanks."

He continued as though I wasn't completely lame, and my heart soared with gratitude and fondness for the man seated across from me.

"My grandfather spent his whole life focused on this island and his research. He didn't have time for a family, which is why I inherited this place after he passed. I always thought I'd end up alone like he did." Henry reached for my fidgeting hands. His touch felt warm and comfortable.

I forced my eyes back up to meet his. "You don't think that anymore?"

He shook his head slowly, his baby blues never leaving my face. "All this was enough for my grandfather." He waved his hand at the island and the bay. "But after meeting you, I knew it would never be enough for me." Perhaps mistaking my wide-eyed look for panic, he quickly added, "Sorry, that's a lot of pressure to put on you. You don't have to say anything. It's probably way too early to say something like that."

Squeezing his hands, I shook my head vigorously. "Henry, I followed you halfway around the world! Your words aren't too much. They are the sweetest thing anyone has ever said to me. And there's no one else I'd rather hear them from more than you."

His shoulders slumped a little, and he let out a loud breath. "Good, good." The smile that lit his face was the most intensely hypnotic one yet. He leaned forward to kiss me once more. It was soft and sweet.

I couldn't suppress the shiver that worked its way through my body.

"Let's get you back inside so you can warm up and put on some dry clothes," he said.

Not wanting the night to end, I held onto his hands for a moment longer. He made no move to let go either. We sat there listening to the waves. The trees rustled in the tropical breeze, and the animals called to one another in the dark, creating the soundtrack to our magical evening. Finally Henry released my hands and rowed us back to shore.

We didn't say much as we walked hand in hand back toward our rooms. Back inside, our wet shoes squeaked with each step across the cement floor. I stopped and Henry held me while I leaned down to remove my soggy footwear. He kept his arm around me as we strolled the rest of the way to the common room. I was sure he could feel my heart pounding as we stopped outside my door.

He turned to me and tipped up my chin, everything tingled wherever his fingertips strayed. I imagined my skin glowing like it did out in the bay; my chin, my cheek, my ear—all lighting up as he brushed a stray strand of hair behind it. Everything seemed to hum with electricity at his touch.

"I had an amazing time tonight." His voice was smooth and soft, like a warm blanket I wanted to crawl under. He leaned in and kissed me with a deep longing I wasn't ready for. All I could do was make an "mmmm" noise, spurring his kiss into a stronger urgency that made my insides melt. By the time we pulled apart, my face was on fire, and I needed to catch my breath.

"Sleep well," Henry's voice was primal and thick.

I could only nod.

He hesitated, and then with what seemed to be a concerted effort, he turned and headed to his room. I stood rooted to the spot, then caught sight of Mort, asleep on the foot of the bed. The click of the door finally got me moving again. I was in a daze as I prepared for bed. Anticipating sweet dreams, I climbed under my covers and soon fell asleep to replays of the evening flashing over and over again in my head.

The next few weeks passed in a rush. Henry was sweet and mostly attentive; however, preparations for our otherworldly visitors were underway, and that took a lot of his time and attention. Many of the other scientists were recruited to help get things ready, too, and Nowhere Island buzzed with an excitement that permeated everything.

We hardly saw Gaël as he worked on his special project to catch the file thief and helped Henry build a satellite that could communicate with our alien visitors. Becca and I settled into a new routine of caring for the animals in The Sanctuary. Abe sent me a large vase full of wildflowers as a "thank you" for assuming his caretaker duties. His note practically gushed with excitement about returning to his first love: research.

Becca often joined Abe when he was working with the dolphins. She even helped make an incredible discovery when she suggested Art's advanced language detecting system might be able to recognize speech patterns in the marine mammals' trills and chirps. With Art's help, Abe created a machine that could communicate with the dolphins. I'd never seen Becca as happy as on the day she was first able to speak with her favorite animal.

The invention definitely piqued my curiosity, so I asked Art if it would work with the various other species on the island. But after some preliminary testings, only the dolphins had a language sophisticated enough to interpret. My dashed hopes for becoming Dr. Doolittle were offset by the progress I saw in the batch of beagles Ross had liberated. These shy, docile creatures who had never stepped foot outside of their metal prison cells were now living the good life and learning what it meant to be real dogs. They romped and rolled in the fresh grass, chasing winged insects and one another. They lazed about in the sun and were always up for belly rubs.

Mort accompanied me most days, frolicking with his new friends. The pack of dogs would often follow me around The Sanctuary as I made my daily visits. Filling the various food dishes and keeping everyone fed and happy took up a large chunk of my day. It also took a while to track down every tagged animal and give them a decent checkup. Though the work was consuming, I was in my element and enjoying it. But my favorite time of day was dusk, as many animals tucked themselves into bed and the nocturnal creatures awoke from their slumber. But the thing I loved most was what happened just as the sun was about to disappear.

I made my way to my preferred spot and spread out a large blanket in the lush grass. It was an open field full of colorful wildflowers, which filled the air with their heady scents. Henry soon joined me, as he did on the nights he could get away from his preparations. We stretched out next to each other on the soft, gray microfiber, and our fingers automatically intertwined like some preprogramed computer code that ran whenever we were in close proximity.

"There!" he said triumphantly, spotting the first firefly as it gradually rose up from the grass. Soon, countless blue lights glowed from all over the field, joining their fellow fireflies in their pilgrimage to find a mate.

I had seen them before, but they always stole my breath each night as I watched them.

"You really need to thank Arlo for bringing them here," I murmured.

He chuckled. "You really love these bugs."

"These aren't your average lightning bugs. They're special. I'm used to normal ones." I tracked one of the glowing dots as it lazily floated through the breezeless air. "I used to catch them every summer on my grandparent's farm."

Henry rolled over onto his elbow to face me. "So your grandparents lived on a farm?"

I followed his lead and turned up onto my elbow. "I spent my summers with them. My mom worked so much, it was nice to actually have someone to eat meals with every day. And I loved working with the animals."

"Is that what made you decide to become a veterinarian?"

I nodded. "Animals are so much easier to understand than people. They don't say one thing and mean another. It's not a popularity contest. You always know where animals stand, in terms of whether or not they liked you."

Henry's smile widened.

I continued, encouraged by his attentiveness. "And animals are always a great judge of character. Especially dogs."

Henry and I both glanced down to where Mort was laying at our feet. He was sprawled out on his back and his pink tongue hung from his mouth as he slept.

"In fact, Mort's the reason I chose to trust *you,*" I said with a shy smile.

Henry raised his eyebrows. "Really?"

"When I gave you the tour of my clinic back in Boston, you mentioned that you'd had Mort since he was a puppy." I picked at some lint on the blanket. "That's when they really form their temperament. A lot of what they are exposed to at that age affects what they are like the rest of their lives. Like in cases of abuse, you'll notice that the animals will turn out timid or aggressive and react poorly to loud noises among other telltale quirks. But if you raise them with love and show them they can trust you as their alpha, then they'll turn out like Mort."

Henry's face was scrunched up, and he was silent as he seemed to consider my words.

I finished my explanation. "Mort is such a trusting, well-adjusted dog. He didn't get that way by accident. It would take a good person to raise him right, for him to turn out the way he did."

"Wow." Henry whistled softly. "I never would have thought of that. That's incredible."

I smiled at him, and then a firefly caught my attention. I watched as it landed on his shoulder. I reached out and let the blinking insect climb onto my hand.

"Has Arlo discovered why these glow blue?" I asked.

Henry watched the bug as it fluttered its wings and rose up into the air over my open hand. "He thought maybe it was the environment or the food supply in the Appalachians. He hypothesized they would revert back to yellow here on the island after a few generations. But that hasn't happened yet."

"So what's he going to do now?"

"Honestly, I think he's forgotten about it." Henry laughed. "They built that low-gravitational enclosure for Timothy and his Komodo, and now all Arlo can think about is his study on insects in lower gravity. Especially the effect on bees, for pollination purposes."

I gave him a funny look, and he chuckled.

"He's always thinking about our first colony on another planet. Don't ever get him started on the importance of insects to our survival; he'll never stop talking."

I laughed along with him. I was about to ask more about the colony when an upset Abe and a sheepish Gaël came out from the tree line and made their way toward us. Henry and I both saw them at the same moment, and we sat up quickly, our hands releasing faster than a junior high couple caught by their parents.

Abe stalked in our direction, and Gaël walked quickly and nervously behind him, rubbing the back of his neck. Abe's gaze never faltered, but Gaël's eyes kept bouncing up to meet ours and then bouncing away. The awkwardness of their lengthy trek made me so uncomfortable that I stood, just for something else to do as we waited for them. Henry scrambled up beside me and shook any errant grass or dirt from his pants. After several more long moments, they were finally close enough, and Abe wasted no time telling us why they had come.

"We found them!"

Chapter 10

It took Henry a moment to catch up to Gaël's topic. Then he replied, "You *found* them?"

Gaël shook his head and sadly corrected Abe's statement. "It would be more accurate to say we figured out what files were missing."

Henry blew out a breath, his cheeks deflating as he released the air. "Okay, well I guess that's a start?"

It was more of a question than a statement.

Gaël shrugged. "I don't know if it's helpful or not, that's why I wanted to tell you as soon as I found out." He waved an arm at our blanket and looked apologetic.

"So what files were they?" I asked.

Abe cut in before Gaël could answer. "They're mine. All the info and research I had from my studies on jellyfish and their longevity. All my years of work, gone! I have to start from the beginning. I can't...." His fists clenched and unclenched by his side, his eyes full of what appeared to be sorrow and a healthy dose of frustration.

Henry frowned and stared at me, but his eyes held that faraway look you get when you aren't really seeing what you're looking at.

Gaël looked from Henry to me and back. "Does that mean anything to you?"

Henry was silent for a moment, then shook his head slowly. "Is there any known connection between Abe's research and Jacob's missing info?"

Gaël grunted. "Jacob is still refusing to say *what* of his was taken."

Henry crossed his arms over his wide, muscular chest. "That man continues to make things more difficult than they need to be."

"Could Jacob be the one who stole everything?" I asked.

"Then he never would have told us in the first place," Gaël answered.

I realized our romantic evening was over, so I picked up the blanket and shook it out. "What if he was trying to throw suspicion off himself?"

Gaël shook his head and absently grabbed the other end of the blanket and helped me fold it. "We never would have known the files were there, let alone missing, if Jacob hadn't brought it to our attention. If he was the one *taking* research.... It wouldn't make sense."

Abe paced nearby and seemed to have a fire building inside him, like a volcano ready to erupt. "I was extremely close to having practical applications to cell longevity," he bellowed. "Not to sound full of myself, but the term fountain of youth wouldn't be inaccurate!"

Gaël nodded, his expression full of sympathetic concern. He opened his mouth like he was about to say something, but nothing came out He quickly pressed his lips together and turned his attention back to his shoes.

"So what's being done to get the information back?" Abe asked.

Henry swatted at his arm and flicked a black smudge from his bicep. "Let's go inside; I'm getting eaten alive out here."

Abe grunted but didn't argue. We followed Henry back inside.

We didn't go far. After entering the building through the double Sanctum doors, we made a left and then right at the end of the short hall. Henry opened the doors to a small lounge area, complete with snack machines, soda fountain, and half-full coffee makers.

"Unfortunately, we were unable to ascertain what was taken or who took it, we could only tell that data was missing. The first time we thought maybe it was a fluke, but Art caught the second gap, and we realized someone was taking files. We still couldn't figure out who was doing it. But we now have a plan in place to catch them," Henry continued, once the door closed behind us in the mosquito-free lounge.

"But only if they steal more files," Gaël added, as he eyed the selection in the vending machines. "Abe's files must have been taken before we set our trap."

"So all we can do is sit back and *hope* the thief takes *more* irreplaceable research?" The calm and laidback Abe I had come to know and like was nowhere to be found. He was now replaced with unconsolable, high-strung Abe.

Henry placed a hand on Abe's arm in an attempt to reassure the distraught man. But Abe was having none of it. He shrugged out of Henry's grip and stalked around us like a caged lion. Gaël pressed a couple buttons and tried to offer Abe the candy bar. Abe swatted at it and stomped away.

"It's the best we can do." Henry's voice was wavering, as though struggling to confine itself to its present octave. "Gaël's plan is ingenious. You should be thankful he thought of it, or you'd have zero chance of ever catching the culprit, which means zero hope of getting your research back."

We all looked at Gaël, who simply nodded meekly, his mouth crammed full of chocolate.

Abe huffed. "Have you even bothered to investigate this? It's a closed system, so we know it has to be someone on the island. Why aren't you interrogating everyone?"

"We can't start a witch hunt over this," Gaël explained, after swallowing what seemed like a painfully large mouthful of his sweet treat. "We start asking people questions, it's only going to cause panic among the innocent and warn the guilty that we're on to them. This way, we catch them redhanded, and we have a chance to find the missing files. If we spook the thief, they may do something crazy like erase everything to hide the evidence."

Abe looked like he might be sick. "You don't really think they'll erase it all do you?"

Henry made a face at Gaël, then shook his head emphatically. "No. Especially if the research is as valuable as you say it is."

Abe's shoulders seemed to relax a bit.

"But that's why we need to proceed with the plan." Gaël's voice was now strong.

Before the others could reply, Art's voice drifted up from everyone's wrist communicators. His thick, warm accent came through like surround sound, and made me feel like I was floating in his words. "Sorry to interrupt. Well, I am not truly sorry, as I do not currently have the capacity to feel regret; however, from my study of human interactions, 'sorry to interrupt' seems to be considered a polite way to interrupt, and so I have chosen to use it now in order to break into your conversation as politely as possible."

I saw Henry's lips quirk up, but before he could say anything Abe called out in surprise. "Who is this?"

"It's Art," I explained. "He's the artificial intelligence program Henry found. That's the voice he uses to communicate with us."

Abe looked unconvinced.

So I did what I usually do and blathered on unnecessarily. "He started out using my voice because he used to call himself Kaly and used feminine pronouns when referring to himself, or I guess it would be herself? But yeah, that just made it super confusing, not to mention kinda creepy. So he chose a new name, Art, and started using masculine pronouns and for some reason a southern accent, though I'm still not sure why—"

"Kaly," Henry finally interrupted me. "I think we're all caught up now."

I grimaced and half shrugged an apology. He smiled and rubbed my arm. "Art, what is it? Did someone try to take more files?"

Abe's eyes lit up at this prospect.

"No," Art replied, dashing Abe's brief hope. "I am contacting you to let you know that the satellite you placed at my disposal has received its first transmission from my hosts."

Henry's wrist communicator squelched as another transmission came through over Art's. Henry pressed a button and beams of light displayed a small video across Henry's arm, even looking at it upside down I could tell who was on the other end of the call.

"Lips," I growled.

"Henry," she gushed, ignoring my outburst. She batted her eyes an obnoxious amount and smiled coyly up at him. "I have some exciting news, and I thought you'd want to hear it first. I've been monitoring the communication satellites and—"

I leaned in so she could see me, albeit upside-down. "We already heard that our special guests have made contact," I interrupted her, unable to help myself.

A twinge of guilt mingled with my satisfaction when I saw the glow fade from her expression. Her face flashed from sour to angry and back to perky and upbeat like an old-fashioned flip-book.

"Well," she forced her smile even wider, "I guess good news travels quickly. Let me know if there's anything I can do to help with the preparations, *Henry*." And she ended the transmission before he could even respond.

I avoided his gaze and instead stared at my shoes, ordering my face to remain cool and blush free. Someone coughed, but I refused to look up to see who it was. I kept my eyes trained on my feet.

Oblivious to the awkwardness, Art once again filled the room with his southern twang. "What she was unable to tell you because she does not speak my hosts' language, is that they will be arriving sooner than anticipated. I gave them your instructions for their planetary approach, and they find these guidelines acceptable."

"S-s-sooner?" Gaël stuttered. "How much sooner?"

"They estimate two earth weeks."

"We won't be ready by then." Gaël clutched at Henry's shirt. "Will we? Can we be ready in two weeks?"

Henry unclenched Gaël's fist from his clothing and punched him jovially in the arm. "We'll have to be. Let's get back to the conference room and see what else needs to be done. Then we'll enlist the help of whomever we need."

His confidence seemed to reassure Gaël; the smaller man's breathing evened out.

"Sorry to cut the night short," Henry leaned in and whispered to me. The warmth of his breath seemed to travel past my face and down to the rest of my body. He kissed me gently on the lips while Gaël pretended not to notice. Abe was still staring and not doing much to hide his ogling, though he could have still been in shock over Art's announcement. It was hard to tell. My own head was swimming with sensory overload.

"My hosts have made a request of their own," Art said, interrupting our goodbyes. "They understand the need for secrecy at this time; however, they have requested that you bring a diverse sample of earthlings with you to the first meeting."

"Come again?" Henry asked.

"I do not understand this command."

"I mean, can you explain that better?" Henry gave the rest of us a questioning look.

We all shrugged in solidarity and waited for Art to explain.

"My hosts understand that you are a community of scientists and therefore the diversity of the sample of humans you will bring with you will be limited to those with a similar background. But they also know that Kaly and Becca are here, as are Tunui and his wife, Amista. My hosts feel they would help give a fuller picture of the human race. They would like very much for those four to accompany you to the first meeting as well."

A quiet followed Art's explanation. Even Henry seemed unsure of what to say.

"I do not understand your silence. Is that an agreement to their request? Do you have concerns, or is there some other outcome I cannot determine?" Art inquired.

"I guess. I'm just wondering why they'd want us along?" I finally spoke into the heavy silence.

"Though they are one species, there are many, what you call, personalities, throughout my host's home galaxy. There is much diversity. So they understand that it is difficult to get the measure of a species by merely studying a small sliver of their population, especially if that sliver is made up of a homogenous group like the scientists here on *Île de Nulle*

Part. Therefore my hosts wish to widen the diversity of your initial group as much as possible and take advantage of the outliers."

"I'm an outlier. Awesome," I said slowly.

"That makes sense, I guess?" Gaël suggested tentatively.

I glared at him.

His cheeks flushed, and he sputtered, "I-I didn't mean you being an outlier made sense; I meant having diversity made sense."

I watched him through narrowed eyes. He gave me a nervous grin and his dimples won me over. My expression softened.

"I think outlier is a pretty adept description." Henry smirked.

My mouth dropped open, and I gaped at him. He started to laugh so I shoved him. He lifted his hands in surrender. "Sorry, I saw my shot, and I had to take it."

"Whatever." I struggled to keep a straight face.

Abe cleared his throat. His demeanor was still on the sour side, though I could hardly blame him. I recalled a research paper I wrote in grad school. There was a mishap in the stairwell of the library after a long work session. My nightly climb out of the archives' dank catacombs at three a.m. ended in my bleary eyes missing a step, and I half tumbled, half slid back down to the closest landing. My ego was bruised more than my body, but the same couldn't be said for my laptop. I actually cried when I realized I had lost months of work. I could only imagine how much worse it was for Abe, whose research sounded much more important and impactful than my study of medication interactions in the average household canine.

He cleared his throat again and waited until he had everyone's attention. "Not to be a buzzkill, but we should probably get going if we want everything ready for their visit."

Henry's smile faded, and a tinge of concern entered the crinkles in the corner of his eyes. "Yeah, let's get to it. We've got a couple of weeks to accomplish what would normally take three months. Piece of cake. Right?"

The next two weeks sped along so quickly it felt like it happened in a single breath. The whole island seemed to come together for the sole purpose of getting ready for our visitors. The lab broke into three camps: a skeleton crew to maintain the lab and two other camps to work on the major problems we needed to solve before the others arrived. Namely, communicating with this new species and making it possible for them to land safely.

Finding available materials that could replicate Art's translation capabilities proved a struggle. Without a direct interpreter, Art's hosts would have to electronically communicate with Art, who then translated it into our language so it could be turned into ones and zeros and finally out through our text-to-speech program, all of which caused rather lengthy pauses. And that worked all right when they were out in space and you could wait hours for their response to spool together into complete sentences, but wasn't ideal for face-to-face contact. Unless they came up with something new, communication would be frustratingly cumbersome.

The third camp handled the issue of our alien friends' landing, which was proving to be problematic. The spacecraft they were traveling in, though capable of flying faster than the speed of light, was *not* built for atmospheric landings. Its bulk was too massive to withstand our gravity. Art informed us that, in their home galaxy, his hosts had atmo-ferries that shuttled them from a planet's surface to their larger vessels in the lower gravity of space.

I will be the first to admit that I have no idea how they solved the communication issue. My eyes would glaze over any time I heard the words they threw around. And the landing issue was solved by some ungodly sized bribes to the most advanced space exploration company in the world and a novel-length nondisclosure agreement that even their grandchildren won't be able to talk about. But somehow, after two action-intensive and somewhat miraculous weeks, I found myself on Tunui's boat, racing toward an abandoned deepwater oil rig to meet honest-to-goodness aliens for the first time in known human history.

Amista sat close to her husband as he deftly steered the speed boat through mostly calm seas. She alternated between wringing her hands and fiddling with the sleeve of her brightly colored blouse. Becca stared off into the distance with a blank expression and only blinked when the wind whipped her hair across her face. "Surreal" was the only word she seemed able to utter for our whole trip to the rig.

As much as I racked my brain, I couldn't come up with

anything to add to her ghostly repetition. And even contemplating our language of more than two hundred thousand recorded words, I couldn't help but think of how inadequate it was at this moment. It wouldn't be the last time my vocabulary failed me.

Chapter 11

The waves crested higher and higher, stretching up toward the rising sun as the oil rig seemed to sprout and grow up from the horizon. Our small boat rose and fell with ever greater lurches that made my heart race and head spin. Tunui was the only one who seemed at ease aboard our vessel. His grip on the wheel was firm but not strained. I tried to convince myself that his stoicism was contagious, but my slow, deep breaths did nothing to calm the stampede in my chest.

The rig grew more foreboding as the minutes ticked by. Its four rust-colored legs were firmly rooted as the sea did its best to rage against them. The two cranes—one large, one small—stood idle against the bright-blue sky along with a tall tower circled in glass at the top. The rest of the platform was flat and unremarkable, aside from the creepy vibe that only an abandoned oil rig in the middle of the ocean could give off.

Tunui pulled in next to another boat that I recognized as the sailboat we took to Mo'orea. Henry left Nowhere Island days ago with the final batch of scientists, who would all be there for the first meeting. He wanted to connect with the advanced team, which had already been on the rig for just over a month; everything had to be triple checked to make sure all was ready. Gaël informed all the non-essential personnel—aka, the four of us on the speed boat—that we didn't have to come until the day of the meeting. Probably to keep us from getting underfoot, or they were worried we might slow down preparations. I couldn't argue with that; I could be a bit distracting at times.

After tying off our boat and dropping the anchor, Tunui reached up and pulled on a thick rope that lowered a ladder on the side of the rig. The rungs were wet and rough. The corrosion under each handhold did nothing to ease my nerves as we climbed nearly two stories up the wobbly contraption. About halfway up, my foot slipped, and I threw myself forward to keep from falling. My chin snapped shut as my jaw hit a lower rung, making a sound like a dulled bell, which no doubt came from the ladder but felt more like it had come from my head. My forearms erupted in angry burns from where they'd scraped the ladder's coarse sides before I was able to halt the decent with my chin. My shins throbbed, and I knew the bruises would be extensive.

Becca had wisely opted to give me a generous head start, otherwise I might have knocked her right into the ocean.

"You okay?" She asked when I finally resumed my ascent.

"Ow," was all I could mutter through clenched teeth as I climbed.

When I finally pulled myself onto the deck of the metal monstrosity, my arms were trembling and my head throbbed. I rubbed my tender chin and turned full circle to take in my new surroundings. Becca clambered up behind me and wasted no time moving away from the edge. Only then did she look around. She kept her gaze from straying too close to the side of the rig. Her fear of heights was notoriously extreme, but being up this high over a turbulent ocean was enough to make even the most secure person a little phobic.

A couple scientists scurried across the open deck with devices in their hands, which they were pointing this way and that. Every so often they yelled out numbers to a third person who typed furiously on his oversized tablet. Becca and I watched them work as we waited for Tunui and his wife to finish the climb. When our little group was back together, we followed the older, tanned man toward the glass-topped tower. He held the door for us, and we stumbled just inside. There we waited a few moments to let our eyes adjust to the darkened interior. In front of us, a narrow staircase split in two. One set of stairs disappeared into the floor to our left, and the second set rose up in a tight, enclosed spiral. I looked up, but no natural light filtered down. Two dim bulbs in small cages hung from the ceiling. No light shone from anywhere else.

Tunui gestured toward the darkened stairs on the left, and we plunged into the belly of the oceanic beast. The air was warm and stagnant as we descended. He produced a powerful flashlight from one of his many pants pockets. His beam guided us down the stairs, which ended in a long hallway. The walls were a dull gray metal that was starting to rust. At the opposite end of the hallway was a partially opened doorway with light and the hum of voices pouring out. We made our way forward as the sound of metal on metal screeched slowly, making my skin crawl. The whole structure seemed to shift beneath my feet, though I couldn't tell if it was actually moving or if I was still experiencing phantom movement that usually happened after an extended boat or plane trip once you're back on solid ground.

Becca was the first one to reach the door; with some effort, she shoved it open. Inside was an impromptu command center. A table in the middle of the room was covered in computers, tablets, coffee cups and empty food packages. There was a large projection of the earth shining on the far wall. In orbit around the globe were smaller lights blinking as they slowly circled. And farther out was a brighter light that didn't blink, it just moved closer and closer to the planet.

"Estimated time of touchdown is less than an hour," one of the scientists said as she bobbed her head between her tablet and the projection on the wall. "We need those measurements from upstairs, now!"

Henry glanced up from his computer and noticed us, he gave me a quick smile and then addressed the scientist. "They should be here any—"

The man with the oversized tablet from up on the deck burst into the room. His face was flushed, and he was out of breath. "I've got the final numbers."

The woman held her hand out impatiently, and the flustered man handed her his tablet. She perched it on the closest flat surface and then began transferring the information from the giant device to her smaller one, her eyes darting back and forth to check her entries as she typed.

I stood quietly with my small group, waiting for further instructions, but everyone was so immersed in their work that no one spoke to us for what felt like forever. It was fascinating to watch them; they talked in some shorthand that made sense to them but sounded like gibberish to me. Finally, Henry stood abruptly, and every eye swiveled to watch him.

"Well folks, I think we've got everything done that we can do before our guests arrive." His smile was genuine but tight. "I wanted to take the time, while we have this brief moment of calm, to thank you for the incredible work you've all done to prepare. I'm honored to be here with you on this epic journey. I can't think of a better group of people to share this opportunity with."

Everyone in the room smiled at one another and began shaking hands with those closest to them. I couldn't help grinning like an idiot as I watched the high-fives and back pats flow. The buzz of voices built as the excitement in the room grew in intensity. It was cut short by a muffled boom, which had every scientist in the room making a mad dash for the door. I grabbed Henry's arm before he could race past me.

"What's going on? What was that?" I asked.

"They've entered atmo." He threw the jargon out, expecting me to understand. "We need to get topside; touchdown will be in about eight and a half minutes!"

Becca grabbed my arm and held me back until everyone else had rushed from the room.

"What are you waiting for?" I practically yelled at her.

"Hey, I'm as excited to meet real live aliens as the next girl," she said, letting go of my arm, "but you don't want to get trampled right before this historic event do you?"

I gave her a look.

She smiled and shrugged. "Come on, you know I'm right, if I had let you go in that rush, you would've gotten hurt."

I blew out a sigh in frustrated agreement. Then waved for her to go ahead of me. She didn't hesitate and was halfway to the stairs before I caught up with her.

Shoving open the heavy door at the top of the stairs, we stepped from the darkness into the blinding light of the noonday sun. It was so bright, I could still see the glowing circle impression every time I blinked. A hand shading my eyes wasn't enough, and I had to squint as I gazed in the direction everyone was looking. What started as a small black dot grew and grew, and soon I was able to make out the shape of a small shuttle.

"Are the cameras rolling?" Henry called.

Only then did I notice two men gripping cameras balanced on single poles; the kind I'd seen my friend, the professional cameraman, use when he expected to move around a lot. The men gave Henry a thumb's up, their eyes never leaving their viewfinders. He got a third thumbs up from the woman on the far side of the platform. She too did it without looking at Henry, her eyes instead bouncing from the drone she piloted, up to the space ship, and then back again.

The minutes slipped by, tracked only by the beating of my heart, until the ship was so close I could make out the logo. It was comprised of the company's name in futuristic letters and a swooping diagonal stroke at the end. This footage would give the lucky company marketing and bragging rights for an absurdly long time.

Henry's excitement reached an agitated state as he paced the length of the rig's decking. "Is the translator operational?" he shouted to three scientists huddled around a machine the size of a microwave, which sat atop a long, thick pole with wheels on its base. It looked like an oversized IV infusion pump.

"Yes," one of them called back. "At least I think so. We ran the tests with Art."

"Art, are you there... or here, I mean?" Henry directed his question at his wrist communicator.

Art's voice came out loud and clear from Henry's wrist. "I will assist in any way I am able."

I stared at his device and then at the one on my own wrist. "I thought these things didn't work off the island?"

"They work like regular watches off the island. *Typically*, they can't do anything more advanced than tell time when you're this far away. Fortunately, Art is anything but typical, so his programing found a way to work even without the island network."

The propulsion engines on the shuttle drew our attention. They flipped so they were firing down as the craft came to hover over the deck of the oil rig. Hot wind whipped at our hair and clothes. The ship lowered slowly, its landing legs extending with one smooth motion. I had to back off to get away from the build up of heat. Those around me backed up too until the vehicle completely settled on its sturdy landing gear. Once the engines were shut down, the scientists couldn't seem to help but scoot closer. I could feel the heat from the deck in the soles of my feet, but it was more uncomfortable than painful. The ship ticked and metal shifted as it cooled slowly in the humid air.

People in khaki coveralls hefted thick fire hoses and sprayed a high-pressure mist across the surface of the shuttle. Steam rose from the ship's exterior like when a cold rain meets hot pavement. The soft sizzling finally faded and the ticking subsided. Everyone around me exchanged anxious glances until the clunk-hiss of a door opening carried across the gigantic, open platform. The sound of the waves crashing below was nothing compared to the sound of my heart thumping in my chest.

Henry came and stood next to me, grabbing my hand and giving it an intense squeeze. I tried to reassure him with a smile, but my nerves turned it into more of a grimace.

Henry laughed. "That's the face you're going to go with on this momentous occasion?"

I couldn't help but giggle and felt some of my tension release. "It's the only face I have."

He threw his head back and laughed, though I couldn't be sure if it was because he really though it was funny or because he was trying to release some tension as well.

"So, not that I know much about spaceships or anything," I began, "But it's kind of a big deal when one lands, isn't it? I'm curious about what story you're feeding to the world. They'd all notice this right?"

Henry's brow furrowed. "Our visitor's ship has a cloaking device that seems to be effective against our tracking systems. Unless someone happens to be looking out through a telescope at exactly the right place in space, they won't spot it. And as for this shuttle," he swept a hand toward the craft with its empty, open doorway, "we borrowed it under the pretense of a few quick trips to space and back for some proprietary tests we made up."

I nearly missed my inaugural alien sighting when I mistook Earth's very first extraterrestrial for nothing more than a hazy bubble. It was the size that made my brain finally register the oddity. Only later did I realized that any bubble on an oil rig in the middle of the ocean was abnormal. Whatever picture I had in my mind about what our visitors might look like, an opaque bubble the size of a bean bag chair wasn't anything remotely close.

Like some invisible force, I was drawn forward. I wasn't alone in my curiosity; I jostled Henry's elbow on one side and Becca's on the other. They, too, had moved toward the floating phenomenon that debarked the ship like clouds.

They were a pearlescent gray, but it wasn't the sun that caused the color shift. It was strange, but it seemed more like they absorbed the sunshine than reflected it. Maybe some internal light source caused the rainbow colors to ripple across the aliens' skin, like a pebble dropped in a lake. And they didn't breathe like I'd come to expect every living creature to do. There was no chest to watch rise and fall, just a large sphere which pulsed like a visible heartbeat.

But the strangest part of all was how every few moments, in the blink of an eye, they would disappear and reappear inches from their previous location, only to disappear and reappear back where they started from. The first time I saw it happen, I rubbed my eyes, thinking it was some optical illusion brought on by the heat and bright sunlight.

Henry must have noticed it too because he asked. "Art, are they teleporting?"

"Like 'Beam me up, Scotty' style?" I interjected.

Art responded from both of our wrist communicators, his voice coming through in stereo. "Their skin is carbon based but also consists of an element you do not have here on your planet. Whereas organic lifeforms on Earth move by using their bodies to transfer energy, my creators can use energy to transfer their bodies."

As if to emphasize Art's point, three of the aliens flickered from one spot to another not too far from where we were standing.

I counted a dozen buoyant, oscillating aliens as Art continued. "They do not breathe in the same way you do. Instead, they collect methane by shooting themselves to another location, thereby surrounding the needed molecules in the new area in order to absorb it. It requires a lot of moving. But your planet has enough of the gas in the atmosphere to keep them going; it was one of the reasons they chose to come here."

Becca rubbed her temples. "Does any one else's head hurt after all that?"

"Are they getting smaller?" I broke in over the nervous chuckles.

"Ah, yes. You will notice they grow smaller when the availability of methane grows less abundant. They will have brought their own supply for emergency situations, no doubt. And they most likely had the shuttle flooded with the gas on their trip here, in preparation for the lower levels. So you will see them begin to shrink as they grow accustomed to your atmosphere," Art explained.

Musical notes filled the air, though it wasn't from any instrument I had ever heard before. One of the bubbles floated away from the rest and closer to us.

"I like it more when they float," Becca muttered. "When they flicker like that, it makes me feel like I'm in a horror movie."

I reached for her hand and gave it a squeeze.

The music was soft and jumbled until the bubble closest to us let out a loud burst of joyous notes.

"Sounds like they brought their own soundtrack, too." I frowned at Henry, but he never got the chance to respond.

The translator box began whirring and clunking, and a progression of lights lit up along the top.

"Welcome to our friendship," a monotone voice verbalized from the box's speaker.

Henry hesitated, cleared his throat and then called out, "Yes, welcome."

More music jingled, an even longer strand of lovely

chords. The translator hummed, and the robotic voice verbalized more words. "Your planet is approachable. Your shape is enchantment. Long collaborate to look forward.

"Um, Art?" Henry raised his wrist closer to his mouth and lowered his voice. "I don't think our translator is working right."

Art's deep voice thrummed from Henry's communicator. "It is translating correctly, Henry. They have not spent as much time and processing power as I have in studying your speech idiosyncrasies and syntax. As with any new language you learn, it will take a while to grasp. They are saying that your planet is very welcoming, your appearance is pleasing, and they look forward to working with you for a long time."

Henry nodded, which made me smile. He caught my expression and seemed to realize his mistake because he went on to answer verbally for Art's sake. "You're right, I shoulda thought of that." Then he raised his voice to address our new friends. "Thank you for making the long journey. We're so glad you have come. We look forward to working with you for a long time, as well."

In a way I swear was deliberately snarky, Art added, "I can assure you that your words sound equally odd to them."

Henry flushed, and all I could do was marvel at the absurdity of it all. Then again, maybe this was normal when it came to extraterrestrial visits; only time would tell.

Chapter 12

It's hard for life to go back to normal after a visit from real, honest-to-goodness aliens. But real life has a way of intruding on even the most exciting adventures. Not that *pedestrian* life on a tropical island was a bad thing. Still, there were animals to care for, chores to be done, and projects to accomplish. So after spending a few hours answering question after alien question, Tunui, his wife, Becca, and I all traveled back to Nowhere Island in order to return to the mundane tasks required of responsible, nonessential-to-the-science-of-an-alien-visit adults.

"Kaly, you're zoned out again." Becca waved her hand in front of my face.

I jerked from my reverie and made an effort to refocus on what I was supposed to be doing. I smacked the bucket of slop against the trough to get the last of the scraps out. The pigs snorted and squealed nearby. My legs throbbed in response, though I couldn't tell if it was from residual pain or from the memory of being trampled. "Sorry," I mumbled. "I just can't stop thinking about it, you know?"

"Really?" Becca's voice dripped with a mock bourgeois

accent. "But meeting aliens is so last year, dah'ling. I simply cannot believe you're still thinking about such outdated things." She patted her mouth and pretended to yawn.

I rolled my eyes but couldn't fight the grin. "You know I've never been the trendy one." I flicked a piece of carrot off the edge of the trough. "But seriously, it's still hard to wrap my head around the thought that we've met *actual* aliens. How do you go back to living your everyday, boring existence after something like that?"

This time Becca was the one to zone out. I let her reminisce as I gently guided her away from the trough, not stopping until she and I were safely out of the gate. This was the one place in The Sanctum, other than the tiger area, that was enclosed in a heavy-duty fence. The pigs, as I was all too painfully aware, could get pretty worked up and were therefore dangerous, and nothing worked them up quite like the anticipation of a meal. Once we were clear, I released the gate holding the pigs back and tried not to lose my lunch as the animals rushed in. I had to turn away; my stomach gave a horrible lurch just from the sound they made as they charged into the feeding pen.

Becca looked from me, to the pigs, and then back again. "You okay?"

I took some deep breaths and slowly nodded at my best friend. "I think I may have a touch of PTSD."

"Not surprising after what happened to you."

"Maybe we can change the subject?" I pleaded.

Her gray eyes gazed heavenward, and she scrunched up her face. Finally, a small smile brushed her lips. "Is it weird that we just met aliens, but all I can think about is Gaël?"

"Yes." I smirked.

She pulled a stick off a nearby tree and flung it at me.

"I'm kidding!" I chuckled, and the knot in my stomach loosened. "Kinda."

Becca threw another stick, and we both burst out laughing as we grabbed fallen leaves, fruits, nuts, and anything we could get our hands on and tossed them at each other. We kept up our war until we were laughing so hard we couldn't breathe; clutching our sides, we reached an unspoken cease fire. One of my legs was soaked and covered in mud from a puddle I was unable to avoid. Becca's hair was disheveled and mixed with twigs and flower petals. She sprawled out on the ground, and I bent over to catch my breath. My heart was finally starting to slow when my wrist communicator beeped. I bit my lip as Henry's name lit up across my dirty arm.

"I can guess who *that* is." Becca's eyes were closed, but she was smiling up at the sky.

I nudged her with my toe. "You'd be right."

She picked herself up off the ground and made a show of dusting herself off. "I'm going to go get cleaned up. Meet ya for dinner?"

I nodded, and she walked off whistling some song Gaël liked to play for her on his guitar. With a swipe through the light beam coming from my wrist, I connected the call and Henry's face materialized as a projected video, with my arm as the screen.

"Hey lovely," he greeted me, then his eyes grew wide with

157

concern. "Kaly, what's wrong? What happened?"

The alarm in his voice caused panic to rise inside me, making me forget I looked the way I did. "What do you mean?" I asked, glancing around frantically.

"What happened to you? You're covered in, in… leaves?"

Realization took a minute, but when I finally figure out what he was talking about, my panic ebbed. "Oh, sorry, Becca and I had a little disagreement and decided to settle it like adults."

His eyebrows rose. "Um, okay, I guess…. All good now?"

I gave him my most innocent look, and his lips turned up in the corners. "Everything's great here."

"Is this something I have to look forward to, when we get into our first disagreement?" He struggled to remain serious.

"If you play your cards right!"

He couldn't hold a straight face any longer; his smile worked its way up to his luminescent blue eyes.

I knew he was busy, but I didn't want the call to end, so I asked the one question I knew would keep him going for a while. "So how are things with our new friends?"

And just like that, Henry's scientist switch flipped, and he forgot about my appearance and why he had called and jumped into explaining all the things they were discussing with our visitors. I listened patiently, fascinated with the stories he told about alien worlds and technology. My attention started to wander when he launched into a detailed explanation of quantum mechanics, but it was like he could read my mind and brought the conversation back to terms I could understand.

"Do you know what I found most interesting?" he asked.

"What?"

"They don't have a word for 'ambition.' It truly is remarkable that they just don't have any idea about it. We even tried to explain it to them, but they couldn't seem to grasp its meaning."

"That's... weird."

"Equally fascinating is the fact that they have like a hundred ways of communicating curiosity." The video quality was so remarkable that I could see Henry's eyes flash as he spoke, and I knew that meant this topic was something that truly piqued his interest.

"I suppose that makes sense." I shrugged.

Amusement played across his chiseled features. "Does it now?"

"If they aren't motivated by ambition, which is hard to fathom by the way, but if it literally isn't in their vocabulary, then something else had to drive them to explore the stars all the way to us. So it makes sense that curiosity is prevalent in the absence of ambition. It can be a powerful thing."

"But didn't it kill the cat?"

"Yes, but satisfaction brought it back," I added with a confident air.

His confused frown made my smile widen. "Is that part of it?"

I pretended to adjust invisible glasses and raised my voice to a nasally, know-it-all tone. "It's the less frequently used rejoinder to the expression. Though the original form of said proverb was actually, 'care killed the cat,' as in worry or sadness."

"Thanks for the lesson, Wikipedia." He wiggled his eyebrows at me; his smile was playful.

I made a face at him. "You know, there's something I've been curious about myself."

"What's that?"

"Do they have a name? Something they call themselves, you know? Like we call ourselves the human race. Do they have a name for their species? It'd be nice to call them something other than 'our friends' all the time."

Henry looked thoughtful. "I've been wondering that too, though it felt a little rude to ask them, for some reason. But maybe I'm just being overly diplomatic. We can ask Art to—"

"I would be happy to assist you with your quandary, Henry." Art's abrupt intrusion made us both jump.

"Sheesh, give a girl some warning next time," I muttered.

"Would you like a chime to announce my arrival to a particular conversation?" Art asked. *The Imperial March* from Star Wars began to play. "Something like this, perhaps?"

I gave Henry a look but didn't comment on how fitting I thought the song was. "Sure, Art," I replied. "That'd be great."

"And to answer your inquiry, I am sure you no doubt heard; their language is musically based."

"Yes, we caught that," Henry confirmed.

"It does not work the way your words do," Art explained. "That is what makes translation so difficult. It is not that each note means a word, it is more that each note makes you feel something, and when you put those feelings together, they communicate what my creators wish to say."

"So they don't actually have a specific *word* for what they call themselves?" Henry guessed.

"Correct."

"Well, can you describe the feeling closest to what they call themselves?" I asked.

"I believe the closest, most efficient description you have would be *musical frission,*" Art replied.

"Frission?" I frowned. "That's French for... shiver. Musical shiver?"

"Goosebumps!" Henry said in triumph. When I gave him a look he continued, "Musical frission is the expression for when you get goosebumps while listening to a particularly moving piece of music."

My eyebrows rose. "I had no idea there was a term for that."

Henry nodded. "But I think it's kinda perfect, don't you? Art, how about Frission? We could call them that."

"I will propose the idea to them. From what I know of their preferences, I believe they will acquiesce."

"Thank you, Art," Henry added quietly.

I said the newly minted name under my breath a few times, to see how it felt. It grew on me the more I thought about it. It seemed to fit them, or at least what little I knew of them. By the time I noticed the silence, it had been dragging on for a while, but Henry seemed lost in thought as well. I wasn't sure if I should speak up or what to say if I did.

My dilemma was resolved when someone said something to Henry off camera that the communicator didn't pick up.

He looked in their direction and nodded. His eyes refocused on me. "Kaly, I've got to go, but I wanted to call you one last time before they take down the network relay. We'll still be here a few more days, but they don't want to risk having the relay up any longer. You can still reach me on the Satphone in an emergency."

"Oh, okay." I tried to keep the disappointment out of my voice.

"It's just a few days, Kaly, and then I'll be home... back."

"It feels more like home when you're here."

The look he gave me was part longing, part satisfaction. It loosened something deep inside me, and I knew the next few days were going to be torture.

Henry's estimate proved inaccurate. I was spreading fresh hay out for the cows when someone came up behind me, scooped me up, and swung me around. I dropped my pitchfork and squealed in shock until I caught the sultry scent of teakwood mixed with a touch of some exotic spice that I didn't know the name of but could recognize in my sleep.

"Henry!" I gasped.

He set me down and spun me to face him, throwing his arms around me once more.

"Hello, lovely," he crooned, his lips just behind my ear.

I sucked in a breath and hugged him back. "What are you doing here? You weren't supposed to be back 'til the day after tomorrow."

His expression grew serious. "We had a... complication

at the rig. We had to haul tail back here so we could figure out how to proceed."

I pulled back from him a bit. "What complications? Are you all right?"

He nodded.

"Is Gaël?" I asked quickly. "Becca would be upset if—"

"He's okay."

"Then what happened?"

Frustration knotted his eyebrows, and he pressed his mouth into a tight line.

"Sorry," I said timidly and then zipped my lip.

"The Frission, they've...." He released me completely and started to pace.

I opened my mouth to ask a question but thought better of it.

Henry reached down and plucked up my fallen pitchfork. He twirled it in the hay. "It seems they've been kidnapped, or whatever you call taking aliens against their will."

A gasp escaped my lips before I could catch it. "Who?" I breathed.

"It's gotta be Pastern. No one else would even think to care about what we were doing with that space shuttle."

"So, they tracked the shuttle to the oil rig?"

Henry nodded and shrugged. "Nothing else makes sense."

"What do we do now?"

"We figure out where they took them and get 'em back." Henry jammed the end of the pitchfork into the ground as if to emphasize his point.

An idea sparked in my mind. "What about Art? Can't he get into Pastern's systems and find out where they're holding them?"

Henry's smile didn't reach his eyes. "For the first time since we found him, Art hasn't been of much help. It's like his capabilities have been cut to a quarter of what they once were. I don't know what's going on. Gaël thinks it might be a security measure in Art's coding—that he goes into a partial shutdown if something happens to his hosts, and that it was triggered when the visiting Frission were taken."

I whistled softly. "So we do this the old-fashioned way."

Henry looked at me quizzically.

"Boots on the ground," I answered his unspoken question. "We find people who work for Pastern and we turn them. It's time for a little Spy vs. Spy."

Henry started nodding before I finished my last sentence. "Yeah, we all know someone who works for Pastern." He noticed my alarmed expression and explained, "It's not like we're all best friends or anything, but they're the largest scientific corporation in the world and this is an island full of scientists. We travel in many of the same circles. The crazy thing would be if we *didn't* know anyone who worked for Pastern."

"Ah, I see."

"We'll put out feelers. The scientific community can be a small world really. And most of them can't keep an interesting scientific discovery a secret to save their lives."

"Really?"

His face finally relaxed. "You wouldn't believe how hard

it was to staff this place! The biggest concern wasn't IQ or education, it was 'how well can you keep your mouth shut' that was at the top of our list of job requirements."

Taking a step closer and filling my voice with as much confidence as I could scrounge up, I replied, "I'm sure we'll find them quickly."

Henry clenched his hands, and the muscles in his biceps grew taut. I reached out to softly touch his arm.

"It's not your fault." I spoke gently, as though not to spook a wild stallion.

His eyes flew to mine, searching them for the veracity of my words. "How did you know I was feeling guilty?"

Absently, I rubbed his arm until his muscles went lax. "Call it a hunch."

"You've got great instincts." He grabbed my hands and pulled me in close.

I let Henry wrap my arms around him and tipped my head back to look up into his eyes. "You're just easy to read."

"Like the animals on your grandparents farm?" He gave me a devilish grin.

Laughing, I nestled my head against his broad chest and listened to his heart beating. It's steady rhythm was reassuring and strong. "Yeah, I like how easy it is with you, Henry. You don't make me second guess myself, or you, or us."

"You are amazing, Kaly Aiton" Henry's voice was almost reverent. "And I have to ask, how are... or should I say were... now that we're an *us*." His words were a bit jumbled, but he pressed on. "What I'm trying to say is, I'm having a hard time believing no one snatched you up before I came along."

"Ah, the age-old question." I tried to play it off like it was a joke, but the look in Henry's eye encouraged me to answer him. "Honestly? I think it comes down to my parents...." I had to swallow down the lump that was rising in my throat. "My dad died protecting my mom from a mugger. My mom said he didn't even hesitate to jump in front of her when the other guy raised his gun."

Henry's eyes widened, and I had to look away or I knew I wouldn't be able to finish. "My mom never remarried. She called my dad her 'once-in-a-lifetime' love." I blinked back tears and continued. "After he died, I used to catch her talking to him at night, like he was still there in the bed with her. They used to fall asleep holding hands, and sometimes when I would go in to wake her up, I would see her hand on his side of the bed. In her sleep, she'd forget he was gone and would reach out for him."

I finally lifted my gaze to meet Henry's. He was nodding, and it gave me the courage to finish. "After seeing love like that, knowing it's out there... I couldn't settle for anything less. It's not easy to find. But knowing what was possible, I kept searching until...."

I held my breath, afraid to finish my thought for fear it would break the spell I felt under whenever Henry was near.

"I used to think it wasn't real." He smiled sadly. "That kind of love. Especially after my mom left. I thought that kind of thing was just fantasy."

"It's not!" I stated emphatically. "I've seen it with my own eyes."

The look he gave me was piercing, longing, magic.

"So have I," he added as he reached back to grab my hands. His fingers intertwined with mine. "Now, I see it too."

And I felt the spell grow stronger.

Chapter 13

"It's like trying to find a needle in a haystack."

Henry and I walked into the conference room to find the discussion already in full swing.

"Yeah, except you don't even know where the haystack is," Jacob muttered. "They could be holing up anywhere; they have facilities all over the world!" He slammed his fist down on the table. "What are we supposed to do, search every single one until we find them?"

He and Lips were seated at the enormous, round conference table. Across from them, Ross, George and two more scientists I didn't know but recognized from the oil rig sat with their backs to us. Gaël paced off to our left, in front of a digital whiteboard that was hanging from the wall. Notes were scribbled and crossed out and scribbled again on the board in glowing red ink.

"We've been discussing the best way to track wherever Pastern has taken the aliens," Gaël explained. "But the only thing we can all agree on is that it was Pastern who took them."

"Actually, Kaly had a good idea," Henry jumped right

into the conversation. "What we need is eyes inside Pastern, and we all know *someone* who works for them. If we all reach out to the people we know and ask a few carefully crafted questions, we might be able to narrow down our search."

Lips watched us intently as we entered, but upon hearing my name from Henry's mouth, the vivacious brunette immediately sat back in her chair, crossed her arms, and let a look of sheer boredom take over her face. "That sounds tedious and like a colossal waste of time."

"Let's hear your brilliant plan then," I sneered.

Henry placed his hand on my arm, and I sheepishly traced a crack on the floor with my foot.

Lips heaved a petulant sigh. "I think we should keep trying to figure out a way to make that scanner."

Jacob scooted his roller chair away from hers before disagreeing. "You read the schematics the AI sent us? We don't have the materials necessary to build one. Earth simply doesn't have the means to make such a scanner."

"And up until we were proven wrong, we thought we were alone in the universe," she countered. "We've got an island full of the smartest people on the planet. There's nothing we can't accomplish if we try."

Henry held up his hands to stop their bickering. "So let's do both. We'll keep trying to build the scanner, *and* we'll reach out to those we know who work for Pastern." He looked around the room. When no one disagreed, he pressed a button on his wristband. "Art, any luck getting through to the Frission's ship?"

"Frission?" Lips raised a perfectly cultivated eyebrow.

"It's what they'd like to be called," Henry explained.

"Since when?"

"It was a recent discovery."

Lips fell silent, but I watched her mouth the word a few times and I begrudgingly admitted that she and I probably weren't as different as I liked to think.

"No, Henry, I have not." Art's voice cut through my thoughts. "If I were capable of feelings, I would tell you I am extremely concerned about my inability to hail anyone aboard the Frisson ship. Something is most assuredly interfering with my signal. I have tried repositioning the satellite numerous times, but I have been unable to get a message through. I will keep trying."

"Yeah, don't bother asking *it* for help," Jacob muttered. "The artificial *intelligence*," he made air quotes with his fingers, "has turned into some sort of halfwit since our visitors disappeared."

Henry ignored him and pressed on. "Does their ship have something on board that could help us track the missing Frission?"

"Yes," Art answered. "They would be able to locate their missing colleagues in cases of emergency. However, it is unknown whether they are even aware that there is an emergency, since I am unable to—"

"We get it," Lips cut him off. "You can't reach them. Which means no access to their tracker. All the more reason to build our own."

"Let's get to it then," Henry added before any arguments could resume.

Since I was neither capable of inventing a scanning device, nor did I know anyone who worked for Pastern, I went back to my work in The Sanctum. Becca went on and on about how great Gaël was and how close they were getting; though, in her defense, she also listened attentively to me gushing about Henry. But with all the animal examinations out of the way, I found I had a lot more free time and not as much to do to fill it. So I approached George about what other work I might be able to help with on the island, instantly regretting it when he turned me over to Lips.

"We need help in the communications room," she informed me. She noticed my blank look and explained. "You know, the room where we first met? Come on, I'll show you."

She took me back to the room where I saw my first pirates, shortly after coming to the island. A man was seated in front of the bank of computers but wasn't paying attention to any of the electrical blinking or beeping; instead, he kept his nose buried in an oversized, hardback book. It looked like a textbook and had "Areospace Engineering" written on the front cover.

Lips coughed loudly and the man jumped, knocking his book to the floor and sending his chair skittering backwards.

"Theo, hard at work again I see?" Lips said, her voice drenched in sucrose.

Theo glowered at Lips and then reached down to retrieve his fallen item. "Nothing's happening, so I was getting some reading done."

Lips eyed the cover. "Boning up on your engineering skills? That would explain why you haven't fixed the sound on the surveillance system yet. It's okay to need a little refresher now and then."

His cheeks reddened. "No!" He seemed surprised by his own high volume. He lowered his voice and continued. "My brother wrote this textbook; I'm just checking it for errors. His head gets so big, sometimes I need to deflate it a little."

"Whatever." She waved a dismissive hand at him and then gracefully sat down in the chair closest to her. She motioned to me to get the other chair and then turned back to the computers. "I've found someone to take your extra shift. You can go, Theo."

He looked at Lips and then over at me.

"I'm Kaly," I said, holding out a hand.

He shook it. "I'm Theo, nice to meet you."

"Yes, yes, blah, blah, niceties over. Now get out, Theo. I've got to teach Dr. Dolittle here how to work the necessary equipment."

Theo's brown eyes rolled up toward his bushy eyebrows, but he didn't reply as he exited the room. And I wish I could say that Lips' instructions were confusing and hard to follow, but she explained everything concisely and in a straightforward way that I was able to pick up easily. It killed me a little how good she was. But it didn't take long until I could handle the communications room solo. Lips stood and was about to leave when she noticed one of the buttons was lit up in bright yellow. She did a double take.

"Theo! That incompetent…." She rubbed her temples. "He forgot to turn off the cell dampener. He always forgets, and I always get the blame."

She shoved the chair out of her way and walked the couple steps so she could flip the switch. No sooner had the light gone out, then her pocket began to buzz and buzz.

"That's weird." She pulled a phone out of her pocket. "No one ever calls me." She looked at me and quickly added, "On my Satphone. Most of my friends are here, and they use their network communicators to call me."

"Mmm hmm," I added, because I couldn't help myself. "Wait, I thought those weren't allowed on the island."

Her glare turned to a smirk. "Only authorized personnel are allowed to have them. And I'm one of the few who's *authorized*." She pressed in a code on her phone.

I waited in awkward silence as she listened. She pressed another button, and the quiet continued. I wandered over to the floor-to-ceiling windows and waited for her to finish.

The sun was slowly drowning, casting its last rays of light up into the sky and out across the endless ocean. A small flock of birds swooped down to land somewhere below the island's lush tree line. One of Abe's beloved dolphins flipped out of the water; I recognized the slightly bent dorsal fin as it caught the light, flashing like a camera before disappearing underwater.

"Call Henry and get him down here quick," Lips ordered.

I turned around to make sure she was talking to me. Though I didn't want her bossing me around, I was torn because I really did want to call Henry and liked having an excuse to do so.

He sounded as glad to have a reason to see me because he didn't even ask why, he simply said he'd be over right over. Sure enough, not even five minutes later he appeared in the doorway of the communications room.

"*Now* can you tell me what's going on?" I flopped down on the seat harder than I meant to and it rolled into the counter so fast it tipped and dumped me out onto the floor.

This caught Lips so caught off guard that she reached out to help me up before she could think about what she was doing. Once I was back on my feet, she realized her mistake and let go of my hand like it was on fire. "I got a voicemail from someone back home."

Henry gave me a concerned look, but I waved him off.

"Not that you'd know this, but I'm from a tiny town in Oregon called Nesika Beach. We don't have any claims to fame other than spectacular views... *and* our very own Pastern facility."

The last part aroused Henry's interest. He took his eyes off me and stepped closer to Lips. "So you know some people who work there?"

Lips nodded. "My cousin."

"What did she have to say?" I asked.

"Nothing," Lips said smugly. "My cousin gave me a whole lot of nothing."

I looked at her uncertainly.

She continued, "The voicemail wasn't from my cousin. Originally, I tried reaching out to her, but she was completely close lipped."

I opened my mouth to say something snarky, but Henry spoke first.

"Then who left you a message?"

"My friend with the Curry County Sheriff's Office. He has some 'news' for me. Whatever it is has gotta be linked to that call I made to my cousin. Can't be a coincidence."

Henry rubbed his chin and stared at a spot on the wall. "Just a message? You haven't spoke to him yet?"

"No." Lips wiggled her Satphone at Henry. "I was waiting for you. I thought you'd like to hear what he had to say." She gave me a wicked grin, and to Henry she added sweetly, "Plus, it gave me an excuse to see you."

"Make. The. Call. Now," I said through clenched teeth.

She swiveled her megawatt smile to me as she dialed.

"'Lo," a man's voice cheerily answered loudly from Lips' phone speaker.

"Howdy, sheriff," Lips replied.

"Ah, you finally got my message. It's good to hear your voice, sugar!"

"Sugar?" I whispered caustically. "As in Sugar Lips?"

"Shut up," Lips whispered to me. Then louder she said, "It's good to hear from you, too, Hobbes. And I'm intrigued about what news you might have to *warrant* a call to me."

"Was that pun intentional?"

"Maybe," she cooed.

"I heard you were looking for information about our favorite facility's latest shenanigans."

"And how, pray tell, did you hear that?" she said at the same time he said, "And I have to tell you, they are definitely up to something over there. Lots of movement and beefed-up security."

He must have heard her question because he answered it without hesitation. "It's a small town, sugar. It's hard to keep anything quiet for long. You know that."

175

"Funny, my cousin didn't mention anything about all that new activity." Lips sniffed. "Apparently she can only keep things quiet around *me*."

"It's Pastern. You know she had to sign a stack full of nondisclosure agreements."

"Still, we're family," Lips pouted. "DNA should trump NDAs."

Hobbes chuckled. "I think lawyers would beg to differ."

"Whatever."

"I didn't hear it from her, either," Hobbes explained. "All my intel comes from the sheriff's office."

Henry circled his finger in the air, giving a 'speed it up' gesture.

Lips nostrils flared and her jaw clenched. It took her a moment to speak. "Look, Hobbes, anything you can tell me about what's happening there would be a huge help."

"Why exactly do you need to know, sugar?"

"You know I hate that nickname," she grumbled.

I could hear the smile in his voice. "Why do you think I use it so much?"

Lips made a face. "Pastern is up to something, something bad. We need to stop them."

"Bad things? Here, in Curry County? You need to tell me what it is, immediately! I'm the law, Kalypso. I need to know if there's bad stuff going down in my jurisdiction."

Lips paused. "I… I'm not sure what it is yet, Hobbes. That's what we're trying to figure out. But *we* can investigate without that whole pesky *probable cause* thing you have to deal with. So if you tell me what you know, I'll tell you what

I know as soon as I get something you can act on."

Silence seemed to create a magnet that drew us all closer to the Satphone.

Finally he spoke. "A large ship came in close to the beach in the middle of the night. Sheriff's station got a frantic call from some teens who were camping nearby. A deputy arrived on the scene. She called the Coast Guard. But before they could get there, the ship was gone. The kids think some rafts came onto the beach and dropped off some crates. They weren't sure what happened after that, but the deputy did arrive in time to see two large semis pulling out. The trucks were followed by a black SUV with all its windows so dark she could tell they were tinted, even at night. The deputy followed them and pulled the SUV over on the premise of the tint but mostly cause her gut was screaming at her that something was wrong."

"When she approached the vehicle, two masked men exited and opened fire with automatic weapons. The deputy was hit a few times. Most stopped at her vest. Still, she was in rough shape when they drove off. Even through all that, she was able to call in the plate." His voice was full of admiration. "Which traced back to a dummy corporation that we're pretty sure is owned by Pastern."

Lips whistled. "Did you question anyone from Pastern in your investigation?"

Hobbes grunted softly. "Not officially. We don't have enough to make the connection that would stand up in court."

"What about *unofficially*?" she inquired. "Did you come

up with anything else that *won't* hold up in court?"

"Only the beefed-up security I mentioned, and more trucks coming and going each day than they've seen over the past year." A police scanner crackled from Hobbes' end of the line. "So if you could find us anything we can use, it would be greatly appreciated. They can't get away with shooting an officer. And if they're up to something worse, I need to know A-SAP."

"Thanks, I'll be in touch." Lips clicked off the phone before anyone could protest.

"You should have at least said goodbye," I admonished.

She stared daggers at me. "Don't presume to know my relationship with Hobbes. We don't say goodbye. We say what we need to say, and then we're done. It's how we do things. Now stop being so judgmental."

I felt my cheeks heat up.

She turned to Henry. "They're in Oregon, I'd bet my life on it. That helicopter that came to the oil rig was short range; there had to be a ship nearby. Once back on the ship, they took that up to the coast and dropped our visitors off on the beach. They had the armed guard waiting to take them from the beach to their compound. It fits."

Henry's face was scrunched in thought. "It wouldn't hurt to take a trip up there and scout things out. It's the best lead we've got so far."

"We actually have one in the works," a new voice added from behind us.

Spinning around, I was the first to catch sight of Ross and ask, "When did you get here?"

He casually leaned against the doorway. "Long enough to hear you mention that you want to check out Pastern's compound in Nesika Beach." He pushed away from the doorjamb and walked over to the large map projected on the wall. He made a motion as though he were grabbing it off the wall and proceeded to 'throw' it to the middle of the room. I couldn't help but gasp as a 3D globe made of light appeared before our eyes.

Ross used his hands to select a spot on the floating orb and spread his palms apart, making the atlas zoom in. He did this a few more times until we had a clear view of the coast of Oregon. "Not-so-fun-fact about Nesika Beach's very own Pastern compound."

He pointed at the location and it zoomed in more until the small town of Nesika Beach was filling the center of the room. It seemed pretty unremarkable, aside from a darkened area just on its northeast border. I thought it was just the program loading at first, but the section remained blacked out even after it was finished rendering.

"They have an animal testing facility at this site. Most of their primates are *there*, in fact."

"Great, more monkeys," Lips said in a not-so-quiet whisper.

Ross ignored her. "They moved all of them over from their labs in Europe when they banned research on primates across the pond."

"Wish they would ban it here too," I added.

"My sentiments exactly, love." Ross smiled sadly at me. He punched a few buttons on the keyboard glowing below the map, and another map popped up. It looked like drone images of a compound, and it fit perfectly over the blank spot on the larger map. "But, in a serendipitous happenstance, I have been planning a trip to free those poor, defenseless creatures from said facility. You are more than welcome to come along and do your snooping while I'm there. As you can see, I was able to get drone footage of their compound, where even our advanced satellites were unsuccessful." He pointed to the new addition to the map. "Dr. Aiton, I would especially enjoy your presence on such an excursion."

"She can take *my* place," Lips huffed. "I've had my fill of monkeys. Lucky made sure of that."

Henry eyed Ross warily. I gave him my most pleading gaze when he turned his attention back to me.

"Yeah, okay," Henry finally agreed. "I'm all for multitasking when the outcome is so beneficial. Why plan one rescue when you can plan two?"

Chapter 14

Like a mighty, slumbering sea creature, the coast of Oregon emerged from its den of mist that swirled in the early morning ocean air. The sun fought to burn off the excess moisture but seemed to be losing the battle. Two-story rocks sat like silent watchdogs in the high-tide waves crashing on the beach. Farther inland, lush foliage peeked out from the top of the blanket of fog, stretching up to meet the clouds hanging low over the mountains.

Our speedboat glided silently closer to the shore. We were nothing more than a phantom, haunting the waters of Gold Beach, Oregon.

"Lips said this is best place to come to shore," Tunui informed us, his accent sounding even thicker this early in the morning.

"How far are we from Nesika Beach?" Henry asked.

"Not far. Ten, fifteen miles."

Ross nudged his way in to the small circle we had formed. I scooted aside to make room.

"Lips' friend Hobbes said he'll have a van waiting for us. Keys are in a magnetic box by the rear passenger-side wheel well." Ross spoke just loud enough to be heard over the waves.

I frowned and jutted my chin at the vast, empty shoreline. "How will we find the van?"

Holding up a tablet, Ross pointed to the map displayed on the screen. There was a blinking dot in the upper-left corner. "He dropped a digital pin. We follow this and it'll take us right to it."

A small splash drew our attention. Gaël was leaning over the side of our boat, holding on to one end of a rope. At the other end was a small, inflatable raft complete with outboard motor.

Gaël spoke quietly but firmly. "We need to move so Tunui can get out of here. This larger boat will definitely draw the Coast Guard's attention if it's here long enough. And Pastern will no doubt be keeping an eye on their reports for a while to make sure we haven't followed them."

Henry was the first to move. He cinched his backpack snuggly against him and then hopped down onto the dinghy. I followed his lead and he made sure I didn't end up in the ocean. Ross came next, with Gaël right behind him. Ross didn't even have the motor started before Tunui was guiding his sleek vessel away from land and out into the open sea. Our new ride was quiet but rather slow, so it took us some time to make it to the beach. We were alone long before we landed.

"I still don't see why we needed to bring Kaly," Henry grunted to Ross as he helped pull our raft up farther onto the sand.

"Thanks a lot," I muttered, checking my bag to make sure it was still secure.

Ross let go of the dinghy, and Gaël and Henry almost fell over from the change in momentum. Putting his arm around me, Ross went on to explain, "I usually have an insider to help in situations like this. Some of the animals in these facilities are intentionally given communicable and sometimes deadly diseases. As much as I want to rescue all of them, I can't, in good conscience, risk exposing our healthy animals to such things. Without an inside man to help identify the disease free animals, I need someone like our knowledgeable Dr. Aiton to assist me with this task."

Gaël and Henry secured the boat among some boulders and tall grass. Upon straightening up, Henry finally noticed Ross' arm around me. I expected Henry to say something, instead he pressed his lips together and drummed his fingers on his thigh.

"If everyone's done talking for me, I'd like to add that I'm a grown woman and I'm here because I choose to be. It'll be fine, Henry." I stepped out of Ross' embrace.

"Will it?" Henry implored. "Do you remember what happened the last time you went up against Pastern?"

Visions of my ransacked apartment and vet clinic crowded in around being kidnapped at gunpoint and the police detective getting shot right in front of me. "Of course I remember."

He threw his hands up in the air. "So I'm just supposed to be okay with you being here right now?"

"But it's okay for you?" I challenged.

Ross cut in. "Wow, Henry, I never pegged you as the chauvinistic type." His voice dripped with sarcasm.

"Shut it, Ross," Henry growled. "Kaly, this has nothing to do with you being a woman and everything to do with you not being able to handle this."

My mouth fell open, and the indignation bubbled up inside me. He grabbed my arm before I could lay into him.

"That came out wrong," he said. "What I meant was, I've had tactical training. I used to teach self defense, and I've done a number of recon and rescue missions similar to this. So has Gaël. And even Ross has managed to bungle his way through more than a few rescues. But you told me yourself that you'd never even seen a gun in real life until Pastern's muscle pointed one at you."

"Well sure, if you're going to be all practical with your arguments," I grumbled.

He reached out for me and I only fought him a little before I let him pull me in close.

"This would be your first time doing field work, and it involves Pastern, which makes it even more treacherous. Call me crazy, but I don't want to put you in their crosshairs again."

"I'll be okay." My words were muffled by his shirt. "Ross needs my help with the primates. It's why I'm here. I'm going to do this."

I felt Henry's whole body stiffen. He didn't respond.

Lights bobbed and flashed from somewhere down the beach, and Gaël interrupted the quiet. "We need to get moving."

Henry let go of me, and I grabbed his arm before he could walk away. "Are you mad?" I asked meekly.

"No, but if you die, I will be."

And as he turned, I swear I saw a smile forming.

The drive to the Pastern Compound was surprisingly pleasant. The ocean stretched out to our left, and the trees and hills climbed up toward the sky on our right. I watched an eagle circle just above the tree tops as we turned down a nearly hidden road.

Henry was behind the wheel, and Ross was giving directions from his tablet.

Ross leaned forward and pointed. "The guardhouse and gate are about a mile down this road, but make sure you don't get too close."

"Oh, you think?" Henry deadpanned. "Then how are they going to see the light-up sign I have on the roof that says, 'we're here for the aliens' if I don't get close enough?"

Ross snorted but didn't respond.

"There!" Henry called in triumph and pointed to an area off to our left that was thinned out enough for a vehicle to fit through. Ross nodded and Henry pulled off to the side of the one lane road. "Get out and tell me when I'm good.

I didn't get the chance to ask him a follow up question; Ross was already out of the van and jogging back to the road. Henry rolled down his window and pulled in farther past the tree line. He only stopped when Ross whisper-yelled that we were far enough.

"We don't want it to be visible from the road," Henry explained. "Just in case."

Gaël slid open the side door and helped me out. Henry met us up by where Ross was hunched over, rummaging through his bag. He pulled out a small, round tin and twisted the lid off. With a few flicks of his fingers he smeared some paste across both cheek bones, his forehead and chin. Then he closed the tin and tossed it to Gaël, who repeated the action. He handed the tin to Henry, who marked his face the same way and then turned with a finger stretched toward me.

"What are you doing?" I whispered, pulling away from his goo-smeared hand.

"It's war paint." Henry wiggled his eyebrows at me.

"For real though," I insisted.

He smiled and reached his finger out again. I let him mark my face as he explained, "It's a special compound that disrupts cameras. This'll make sure they can't ID you later."

"I don't know whether to be scared or impressed," I remarked. "Though I will say, I'm glad we're on the same team."

We made the rest of the trip on foot and without uttering a word. I felt pretty secret-agency when Henry and Ross used hand signals, and I managed to follow what they were trying to communicate. It was surprisingly easy to slip past the guardhouse and fence. I almost mentioned this to Henry but decided to keep my concerns to myself. Ten more minutes and we arrived on the outskirts of the Pastern compound. The buildings were painted in greens and browns and clustered close together. Large, leaf-covered nets spread out overhead.

Henry finally broke the silence when he pointed to a far building that was being guarded by men with automatic weapons. "If I were a betting man, I'd say the Frission are being held in there."

"You know how I live to disagree with you," Ross quipped. "However, this time I think you're right."

I held up an angry hand to stop the fight before it started. "So what's the plan?"

"Kaly and I create a distraction, and Henry and Gaël go in and rescue our extraterrestrial visitors."

"And what is this distraction?" Henry asked sternly.

Ross dabbed at the paste on his face as if to make sure it remained in place. "A little madcap monkey business." He grinned.

I blew out a slow breath. "So freeing the primates is the distraction, but *how* exactly are we supposed to free them?"

"We'll need a truck, the keys, and possibly the alarm codes. Though if we're lucky, they won't have alarms."

"Oh, is that all? Piece of cake," I retorted, mumbling, "If we're lucky."

"Yep, that's what we did last time."

"This plan has worked before?" Henry was incredulous.

I gaped at Henry. "That's the question you want answered most?"

"Yes." Ross shrugged. "Well, up until the *getting away* part."

"So it didn't even work before, but you think it'll work now," I said as more of a statement than a question. "And how are we supposed to get all those things?"

"Lips mentioned a coffee shop nearby where the employees like to spend time when they aren't working," Ross explained. "We'll go there and lift some keys, make duplicates, and return them before anyone's the wiser. A few casual questions and we can determine if they have alarms."

My doubtful look didn't faze him.

"I'm very charming." He fluffed up his thinning, dark hair. "I've talked ladies out of more than that before. This shouldn't be too difficult. And if that doesn't work, we'll go to Plan B."

Gaël finally joined the conversation. "What's Plan B?"

"We'll cross that bridge when we come to it." Ross waved a hand in dismissal.

"I already see a flaw in your plan," Henry countered.

Ross chewed his cheek, as though to stop himself from rising to Henry's bait.

"See that?" Henry pointed to a pole situated at the edge of the compound. "Surveillance cameras. You didn't mention how we get past those in that *comprehensive* plan of yours."

Ross squinted, his head tipped to one side. "Gaël, my kind sir, this appears to be your department. How do you suggest we get by them unnoticed? Unfortunately my paste only scrambles our faces, it doesn't render us invisible. Though how awesome would that be?"

Gaël produced a handheld device out of his bag. I recognized it immediately as the EMP cannon Henry used to stop whomever was following us on our trip back from Mo'orea.

"We knock out the cameras with this. And who wants to guess where their first priority will be when the panic sets in?"

"They'll want to secure the Frission. They'll assume we're here for them," Henry answered begrudgingly.

Gaël nodded, excitement sparkling in his dark-brown eyes. "And when they go there to secure the Frission, Kaly and Ross can get as many of the monkeys onto the truck as they can. Then, once they're away, we alert the guards to the missing animals and...."

I finished his thought. "When they see the primates are gone, they'll think we were just a group of animal activists and will let their guard down over where they're keeping the Frission. Then Henry and Gaël can go in and rescue *them*."

"They're going to pursue you," Henry stated flatly. "Once they see the animals are gone, they'll follow the truck. How can you be sure you'll get away?"

"We can tip off Lips' friend in the county sheriff's office," I added enthusiastically, feeling the excitement of a plan coming together. "We let him know that Pastern's goons are likely to surface outside of the compound, and maybe the Sheriff can take care of that little problem for us. Win-win."

Henry shook his head slowly. "So much can go wrong. I don't like it."

"Do you have a better plan?" Ross challenged.

Henry brooded but didn't reply.

"Didn't think so." Ross sniffed. "So we go with this plan, if anything goes wrong, you deploy the flash-bangs we brought, and you get out of there as fast as you can. We all meet at the rendezvous point as soon as possible and call Tunui as we're motoring out to meet him. Though we'll probably need something bigger than that dinghy we came in on, if there are a lot of primates. Leave that to me as well."

Henry opened his mouth like he was going to say something, but Ross didn't give him a chance; he had already started walking back toward the van.

I grabbed Henry's hand and tugged him along after me, following Ross but staying out of earshot.

"I've learned not to ask 'what's the worst that can happen?' in situations like this," I spoke quietly but as confidently as I could manage. "And to just hope for the best and take it all as it comes."

"That doesn't make me feel better about any of this," Henry grumbled.

I turned to look at him only to miss a tree branch in front of me. It clobbered me in the back of the head and sent me careening into his arms.

"If that was supposed to instill confidence in me, it didn't work." His lips twitched at the corners.

I smiled sheepishly as I rubbed the back of my head and untangled myself from his arms and my hair from the offending tree branch. "I'm just getting my maladroit tendencies out of the way now. So I'll be totally adroit when I need to be."

"Right," he said with a frown, but he grabbed my hand again and his steps seemed a little lighter.

The coffeeshop hummed with the activity of a late-afternoon rush.

We had spread ourselves out around the cafe, to better our odds of finding a good candidate for Ross to "charm." I was on my fifth cup of coffee and practically bouncing out of my seat when Henry and Gaël rejoined me. They motioned for Ross to come over as well.

"We've been here all day, and I haven't overheard a single conversation that sounded even remotely promising," Henry lead the discussion.

Ross rubbed his eyes and then stared sullenly at the table, not uttering a word.

"Should we wait longer?" Gaël suggested. "Or come back tomorrow? Oh, or does anyone know how to pick a lock? Maybe we could do that instead of trying to lift someone's key."

"We don't know if there are alarms or not," Henry reminded him.

"I could go back and look for the box that would power the alarms," Gaël offered. "Then I can knock that out with the EMP too."

A young woman approached our table. "Dr. Smith?"

I jumped a little when she spoke, more from coffee jitters than from being startled.

She had dark-brown hair that was bleached blonde and pulled back into a tight bun. A white lab coat was slung over one arm, and in her other hand was a cup with a fluttering tea tag dangling from a string. "Dr. Smith," she said again, this time with certainty as she stared straight at Ross.

Ross did a double take. "Summer?"

Her smile lit up her whole face. "I thought that was you!"

"What on earth are you doing here?" Ross blurted out.

"I'm working up at Pastern now. I like to come here for some chamomile tea when I finish working; it helps calm me after my shift."

"You know her?" Henry's voice was calm but I could sense the agitation just below the surface.

"I, uh, yes, Summer and I go way back." Ross seemed to sense Henry's agitation, too, because he quietly added, "I had no idea she was working here."

"Do you enjoy working for Pastern, Summer?" I asked, but before she could answer I asked a second question. "What do you do there?"

"I hope you didn't ask anyone else questions like that," she didn't try to hide her sassiness.

I sputtered and felt the blush start to rise.

Henry quickly answered, "We haven't talked to anyone."

Summer sipped her tea and then replied, "I'm not surprised. Everyone at our compound was just warned to keep their mouths shut, especially after your little visit this morning."

Henry's face was stoic, but my worried glance gave us away.

She continued in a quiet voice. "So my assumption was correct? You were the ones trespassing at the compound early this morning?"

"What makes you think—" Ross started to say, but Summer cut him off.

"They made an announcement this morning. Some nonsense about corporate espionage and how we all need to keep our mouths shut when we're outside of work. And that if we see anyone lurking around we're supposed to report it immediately."

Henry groaned and shifted in his chair. "This complicates an already ridiculously problematic plan."

"Well, then you're awfully lucky I'm here." She finished her tea and threw her cup away.

"So you followed my advice?" Ross pointed to the lab coat slung over her arm. "You're a scientist?"

"I'm just waiting for my *endorsement*." Her smile was for some private joke I didn't understand.

Henry halfway stood. Apparently he wasn't quite as clueless as I was. "What's she talking about, Ross?" He demanded.

"It seems once more the fates have aligned," Ross marveled.

"More like I knew you'd eventually come here, and I thought I could help you again… only this time with a much happier ending." She and Ross exchanged a look that I didn't understand. "And then maybe I could be reunited with Lucky?"

Now it was my turn to stand. "You know Lucky?!"

She turned her dark eyes to appraise me. "*You* know Lucky?"

"What's she talking about, Ross?" Henry repeated himself.

Ross embraced the young lady and kissed her on the check. "I can't tell you how glad I am to see you. You help us out, and I'm betting a couple other people will be giving you a recommendation too." He jutted his thumb at Henry and then Gaël.

Summer's smile widened even further. "Excellent! Let's go save some primates. That is why you're here, right?"

Henry's face was growing redder by the second.

Ross held up a hand to stall Henry's tirade. "Calm down, Henry. She's the one who rescued Lucky. She was my inside man… er, woman. She's been wanting a job at our facility ever since. I think she's planning on this being her audition."

"You told her about our facility?" The ice in Henry's voice could make a polar bear shiver.

"Only that it was a place where we made discoveries to benefit humanity. Ones that didn't come at the expense of animals." Ross looked Henry in the eye.

Henry was silent for a moment, though I couldn't tell if he was considering Ross' words or counting to ten to calm himself. Finally he said, "I don't know if it's a good idea to involve her. This is going to be dangerous; I already have Kaly…."

The look I gave him made him swallow the end of his sentence.

Summer was undaunted. "Trust me, you'll want my help." She smirked at Ross. "And a wise man once told me, a little fear is good, as long as you don't let it overwhelm you."

Chapter 15

"If you want to pull this off, you're going to follow my plan," Summer insisted.

"*Your* plan doesn't account for the second half of *our* plan," Henry argued for the umpteenth time as we stood around a large box truck with the logo of a local laundry company painted on its dull-gray sides.

Summer sighed and picked at the peeling paint on one of the truck's front fenders. "You're really sticking to your alien story?"

Henry grunted but said nothing as he squinted into the early afternoon sun.

Neither the truck nor the abandoned warehouse we were standing in front of offered any shade. I was dripping sweat, and the drab uniform Summer gave me to wear was stiff and sticking to me in all the wrong places. I tried to lean nonchalantly against the laundry vehicle to hide my discomfort. Upon pressing my hand to the slick, metal surface, the sweat on my palms turned the truck into a Slip 'N Slide, and before I knew what happened, I was flat on my side with gravel sharply digging into my leg and arm.

Ross quickly stooped down to help me up. My fall managed to stop Henry and Summer before they could circle back into the umpteenth-and-one round of their argument.

I brushed gravel from my now-dusty uniform. "So we compromise. We do Summer's plan for the first half and the plan we came up with for the second half."

"I'm all for getting those poor animals out," Henry insisted. "But rescuing the Frission has to be our priority here."

"The only difference between your plan and my plan," Summer's voice was syrupy sweet, "is that at least my half of it is guaranteed to work."

"You're cockiness does nothing to ease my concerns." Henry's eyes appraised me, and I gave him a short nod to let him know I was all right.

"It's not cockiness," Summer stopped picking at the paint and looked up at him. "It's confidence."

He held a hand up to shield his eyes so he could look at her. "What's the difference?"

Her back was to the sun, so she had no problem locking onto his gaze. "The fact that I'm right."

They held their staring competition until the sun became too much for Henry and he had to look away. He forcefully shoved his hands into his pockets.

"I think she's right." I finally broke the weighted silence.

Henry's mouth fell open.

"I'm sorry, but she's been planning this for a lot longer than we have." I couldn't bare to look at him, so I squinted at the ground and pretended the sun was keeping me from looking up. "We get the primates out. Once Pastern realizes they're gone, the focus will shift to that, and that's when you move in to rescue the Frission."

"Sorry, Henry, but I agree," Gaël added. "I think it's our best shot. And it's not much different from *our* plan."

"Except the primates will be gone before they even realize it. It won't be as chaotic as we need to it be." Henry pulled his hands out of his pockets and waved them as though to emphasize his point.

"So making a mess of everything was part of your plan?" Summer said it as more of a statement than a question.

"Enough!" Ross shouted, then took a minute to compose himself. "We're doing Summer's plan. Henry, if you don't like it, you can sit this one out."

Anger flashed in Henry's eyes. He clenched and unclenched his fists a few times before speaking again in a quiet voice with a razor-sharp edge. "If you think I'm going to let you all go in there without me, you're mistaken. But when this goes sideways, and it *will* go sideways—"

"We get a big fat 'I told you so' from you. Got it." Ross' cheeriness felt a bit too forced.

"Stop talking before I leave you all here to figure out a new plan without your laundry truck," Henry snapped. He turned on his heel and stalked toward the driver-side door.

Before anyone could say anything, he yanked the door open and climbed into the cab. The aggressive rumble of the engine made the plan and what we were about to do seem much more real.

"He won't really do that will he?" Summer asked, her

eyes darting back and forth between the truck and me.

"No." I tried to sound more confident than I felt. "I don't think so," I added quietly.

We all looked up into the truck's cab, and Henry made a "well, what are you waiting for?" signal with his hands.

That got us moving. Ross moved to the driver's door and swished his hand at Henry until Henry begrudgingly scooted across the bench seat to the passenger side. Summer, Gaël, and I climbed up into the back of the truck. She led the way around large carts piled with stacked, clean linens and pulled open a panel that gave way to the secret compartment. It was next to impossible to notice that the box trailer was actually just over a foot longer than the inside storage area.

"Remember, we're doing the first part of the plan my way, so they're going to give me a head start." Summer gave us the once over. "See you soon," she flashed a smile as she closed us in.

Her footsteps grew faint and were followed by a hollow racket of the large back door rolling down. The muffled ka-chunk of the metal latch being locked into place felt a bit too permanent. I'm not one who struggles with claustrophobia, but being stuck there, in the dark, made my heart race and my hands even more slick with sweat.

There was a muffled squeak as a door opened and slammed shut somewhere behind me, and I hit my head as I turned toward the noise. My stomach churned as the truck started to move, and I wanted to kick myself for not facing forward when I climbed into our hidey-hole; only, I couldn't moved more than a few inches. I tried to find a comfortable position, but standing ramrod straight for any extended period of time is rough.

My mind wandered back to the last two days we'd spent locked inside a musty, seaside motel that charged by the hour. Even the long walks on the beautiful beach weren't enough to keep the four of us from going a little stir crazy. But Summer insisted we hide out there until laundry day so we didn't arouse the suspicions of the small, close-knit community. The skin on the back of my neck started to tingle, and not in a good way, when I thought about the motel's less-than-pristine sheets.

Changing my train of thought wasn't easy and only led me back to thinking about my discomfort. My feet soon went numb, so I did my best to bounce on my toes to wake them up. It only worked slightly, and I was about to groan in frustration when Gaël beat me to it.

I felt him shift in the cramped, dark space next to me. He was bigger and would be able to move even less than I could. I didn't envy him, and the thought of it made my discomfort a little more bearable or perhaps a bit less miserable.

"Hang in there," I murmured. "We'll be there soon."

Another grunt was his only response.

We made a careful turn, and I was startled by the scraping and metallic banging of what I assumed were trees hitting the sides of our truck.

"It's the road to the compound, right?" Gaël's question was more like begging.

"It's gotta be."

We rumbled far too slowly the rest of the way, pausing briefly at what must have been the guard's station. I held my breath as muffled voices exchanged unintelligible words. Gaël was whispering something over and over too softly for me to make out.

Muffled voices grew louder when the back door opened. I thought my lungs would explode as Gaël and I waited, neither of us moving a muscle.

We both let out audible sighs when the door was rolled back down and two hollow thumps sent us on our way.

"So far, so good," I couldn't help smiling.

"Don't jinx it!" Gaël ordered.

My breathing grew shallow as we once more pulled to a stop. I wiped my hands on my starched but now slightly dusty uniform and banged my knees as I attempted to march in place. The tingling from my toes had moved up to my calves and was mixing with my adrenalin to make a horrible sensation in the lower half of my body.

An eternity later, I heard the lock thunk open and the door roll up. I counted to ten and slowed my breathing. Light flooded into our confined space, and I had to blink a few times before I could make out that the blob who'd opened the door was actually Summer.

Her grin was mischievous, and there was fire in her green eyes. "So far, so good."

"Don't jinx it!" Gaël and I said in unison.

Her smile only grew wider. "Let's go save some lives."

We emerged from our tomb on wobbly legs. Henry was there to help me climb down from the back. He handed a pack to Gaël and gave me a quick peck on the cheek.

"Stay safe or you'll be in so much trouble. You hear me?" Concern filled his piercing blue eyes.

I nodded. "You too." I hugged him hard.

"If they have your aliens here, they'll be keeping them in the building just across the quad." Summer pointed off toward a grassy area in one direction, then turned to face the loading dock where we were now parked. "The animals are in here. So this is where we part ways."

"And you're sure they're using the Enoch System to run all their buildings' security?" Henry asked.

I thought their former argument was about to start again, but Summer just sighed and responded, "The security techs all love to brag how it's the best system out there. Top-of-the-line and worry-free are the words they love to use the most about it. Honestly, it's made them all a bit lazy if you ask me."

Gaël nodded solemnly, but then a wicked smile lifted the corners of his mouth. "It would be worry-free... unless someone happened to know of a class break for the Enoch system. Lucky for us, I happen to, which is unlucky for them."

"What's a class break?" I asked.

He took a deep breath like he was about to tell me but then let it out again. "It would take a while to explain, maybe another time."

Before I could respond, Summer shoved a small flip phone into my hand. I turned it over, marveling in what many, present company especially, now considered to be obsolete technology.

"They're burners, but they aren't secure." Summer handed one to Gaël too. "Only use them if it's a worst case, no other options, you're about to die, situation."

I frowned and was about to question her, but the fierce look in her eye made me hold my tongue.

"In and out," Summer added. "The faster the better. Let's get moving."

Henry led Gaël off to skirt the edge of the grassy quad, ducking behind trees and bushes to avoid detection by any of Pastern's employees who may have happened to pass by. We watched in silence until they were out of sight.

Summer's words broke us from our vigil. "The launders' code is Tango, seven, Foxtrot, Zulu, two, Bravo, nine, nine. It'll open the bay door, and you can back the truck in. Just give me five minutes to get to the cafeteria and swipe my badge. I don't want to give them any reason to suspect me."

Then she was off, and we waited six minutes just to be safe before I punched in the code. Ross backed the truck in, and the race to save the primates was on. Everything was going without a hitch, which only gave me time to worry about Henry and Gaël. The research lab was closed on laundry days, so we were able to move about without fear of interruption. I worked as quickly as I dared to sedate the animals that Summer had indicated by a blacklight reactive symbol on the outside of select cages. We couldn't risk taking any of the infected animals, so Summer had carefully marked which ones were safe to remove. I was pleased to see that most of the cages held the glowing mark.

Ross helped place them gently into the laundry carts, and

then we quickly wheeled them into the truck. It felt like no time at all before they were all loaded. We unfolded and mussed up the clean linens to make them look like they were simply the piles of dirty linens the company usually left with, then surveyed our work to make sure there were no signs of our stowaways sticking out from under the carefully piled cloth. With one final, silent prayer, I closed the door and we got into the cab. I snatched up the hat Henry had left behind for me. It still smelled like him, teakwood and mahogany, a scent that drove me crazy.

"Stop sniffing it and put it on," Ross barked.

I snorted nervously and tucked all my hair up inside the hat and lowered the brim over my face as much as possible.

Ross seemed to sense my apprehension. "The guy at the guard station didn't even look at Henry; I'm sure he won't notice you're not him. He probably couldn't even see him from down on the ground. Just keep your head low and we'll be okay."

The last part of this plan involved hoping that the guards missed that I was different from the person who came in earlier. It was risky, but there wasn't much room in the secret compartment, and Gaël was significantly smaller than Henry, so he got stuck in purgatory while Henry got the front seat.

It also meant that since Henry would be off freeing the Frission, I would have to fill in his spot in the front of the truck when we left. It would be far more obvious if the truck came in with two people but left with one.

"Breathe," Ross commanded as we rolled to a stop at the guard's station.

I ducked my head more but tried to force my breath in and out evenly.

A warm breeze blew int0 the cab as Ross lowered his window.

"Took a little longer than usual today, huh?" the bored guard called up.

I risked a peek and was encouraged to note that I couldn't see the guard from where I sat. *Don't climb up here, don't climb up here.* The mantra seemed to echo as it dashed back and forth through my frantic thoughts.

"You know how these scientist types get." Ross' voice was so calm and jovial, I couldn't help but marvel. "They like to make big messes and then expect the rest of us to clean up after them. Am I right?"

This elicited a chuckle from the guard somewhere down below Ross' door. "You know it! Just gotta check the back and then you can be on your way." He sounded almost apologetic.

"No worries, man. We all gotta job to do. I get it," Ross replied.

I held my breath as I listened to the latch release. I suppressed a shudder as the vibrations from the door rolling up seeped through my seat. A drop of sweat trickled down my neck from somewhere under my hat. Ross' hand came over and clamped down on my jostling knee.

"Sorry," I mumbled and made the concerted effort to stay still.

"Be cool."

"What if he looks under the sheets and towels and stuff?"

"Would you stick your hands into dirty laundry at an animal testing research facility?" Ross scrunched his nose, and I couldn't help but giggle as the nerves bubbled up inside me.

It took all my willpower not to screech when the door slammed down behind us. My heart resumed beating when the latch clunked into place, and two loud thumps were our signal to depart. Ross waved his arm out the window and then shifted the large truck into gear. I stayed low in my seat until we were down the facility's private drive and back onto the safety of the oceanside highway.

I ripped off my hat, letting loose my shoulder-length hair. I smacked Ross with the hat playfully and he gave a celebratory "whoop" as we sped along to where our boat was hidden. The first part of the plan had happened exactly the way Summer said it would. She would no doubt rub it in Henry's face extensively.

The sudden thought of Henry made my good mood short lived. Ross seemed to sense my abrupt change, he eyed me quickly between longer periods of watching the road.

"They'll get it done," he said. His tone was confident and reassuring, though after his convincing act with the security guard, I was less inclined to believe him. "Don't worry, they'll be fine."

I took one more deep breath to steel my resolve, and then sent the coded 'all clear' message to Summer to set into motion the second part of our plan. With nothing left to do now but wait, I stared out the window and tried not to think about all the things that could still go wrong.

The ocean waves crashed violently against the shore as a storm raged farther out to sea. My heart crashed violently against my ribs as we drove farther from Henry and Gaël. The plan was for Gaël to get into the facility where they were keeping the Frission and get them out, while Henry commandeered an escape vehicle from the employee parking lot. And while they were doing that, Ross and I would get back to the boat he'd purchased and transfer the anesthetized primates. I didn't bother to ask him how he managed to get the boat; I knew it would only feed his already oversized ego.

After dropping Ross and the primates off, I would drive the laundry truck back to the warehouse to meet up with Gaël and Henry. We would then follow the highway up to a small airport about an hour and a half north of Nesika and leave the truck there to make it seem like we'd made our escape by plane.

It felt as though the plan could work, especially after our success with the first half of the rescue mission. I tried to think good thoughts as we carefully transferred the animals to the boat. I checked their vitals and administered another dose of anesthesia to each of the slumbering beasts.

"That should keep them asleep until you get to the next port. Summer said the crates will be waiting for us there." I nodded at Ross.

"I'll be more at ease once we have them secured in those cages. I must admit, it makes me a bit nervous to have them loose like this. Especially since I'll be by myself."

"We'll get there as soon as we can," I assured him. "But the anesthesia will last long enough, I promise. Just head straight there and load the crates onto the boat. You'll be able to get them safely inside long before they wake up. And make sure you put the ones with black bands in crates by themselves."

"They're the potentially aggressive ones?" Ross asked, an eyebrow cocked wearily over one eye. He nervously glanced over his shoulder.

"Only if they wake up trapped in an unfamiliar place with another primate they aren't used to. So get them in a separate crate and everything will be fine," I reassured him. "We'll meet up with you and be on our way in no time."

I stepped into the cold ocean to help Ross launch the boat. The waves did their best to work against us as we shoved the craft away from the beach. My heavy boots crunched hard into gravel as I dug in each step. A few more pushes and he was finally able to pull himself aboard. A quick tug on the motor and he was on his way. I worked my way back up onto the shore and watched until he was out of sight, then returned to the laundry truck for my trip back to the warehouse. After hauling myself up into the cab, I tried to find a comfortable position, but the springs in the bench seat made it difficult. Adjusting the mirrors and figuring out where all my controls were located took a few moments but my anxiety made it seem to take much longer.

I was picking up speed as I turned onto the highway that would lead me to the rendezvous point, when the burner phone rang. The sudden noise scared me long before I remembered Summer's warning about the phone. My hand shook as I flipped it open and stabbed the button to accept the call.

"Kaly, we have a problem," she nearly shouted. "A big one!"

Chapter 16

My heart dropped to the floor somewhere near the pedals, and I'm pretty sure I stomped on it in my search for the brakes. A car behind me honked aggressively as it swerved to avoid slamming into me. I regained my composure long enough to pull the truck over to the side of the road. A few unfriendly fingers waved at me as upset motorists passed by.

I ignored them as my focus honed in on Summer's words.

"What's the problem?" I all but yelled back at her.

Somewhere on Summer's end of the line, I heard muffled commands being called out. I had seen enough action movies to know what automatic guns being cocked sounded like, and that sound traveled through loud and clear as I listened in abject horror.

"Summer, what's wrong?" I slammed my hand against the steering wheel.

"They were right; they needed more chaos," she whispered.

My head dropped, no longer capable of holding itself up. "Pastern knows Henry and Gaël are there?"

"They're trapped inside the—" Her voice cut out.

"Summer! Summer!"

It took me a moment to find the speaker button, but then I dropped the burner on the seat next to me and threw the truck into drive. "Summer, I'm coming, but you need to tell me what's happening!"

I pulled out in front of a silver SUV and paid no attention to their honks of protest or the screeching tires—slamming my foot down on the accelerator and not stopping until it hit the floor.

"Kaly, you can't come back here." Summer's voice finally came back through my phone's speaker.

"I can't just leave them trapped!"

"It's time for Plan B."

"We don't have a Plan B!" I leaned forward in my seat as though that might make the truck move faster.

"Then we need to come up with one quick. Everything is going to he—" Her voice cut out again. Maddening silence filled the air for a few seconds before I could hear her again. "I don't know what to do! The guys with the guns aren't talking about taking prisoners, Kaly. They're talking about collecting bodies."

A buzzing started in my ears, and my vision started to tunnel. I shook my head and gripped the steering wheel so tight my knuckles turned white and pain shot up through my wrists.

"Burn it to the ground." The words were out of my mouth before I had a chance to process them.

"What?"

"You heard me, light it all up!" I let the anger, fear and

frustration course through my words. "They need chaos, let's give them some."

There was the briefest of pauses and then her response came.

"My cover will be blown."

"We'll figure that out once everyone is safe. Please, Summer," I begged.

"I won't go near the animal lab; I can't hurt those poor creatures we had to leave behind."

"Focus on the places closest to where Henry and Gaël are. That should help give them some cover."

She growled. I could practically feel her vexation through the phone.

"Fine," she said, just before she hung up.

I scrambled to pick up my phone as the line went dead. I hoped Summer would be able to do enough damage to make the next part of my impromptu Plan B successful. With one hand I kept the truck steady, and with the other I dialed 911.

"I need to report a fire."

The firetrucks' sirens snapped me out of my frenzied drive back to Pastern. It was enough to keep me from turning up the private drive. Instead I pulled over to the side of the road, near a cut out in the dense trees just big enough for my truck to park safely. I watched the two noisy, red giants rush past me and toward the location I had dispatched them to, willing it to be enough to give Henry and Gaël a chance to escape.

The emergency phone sat painfully silent on the seat next to me. I glared at it, making idle threats as it refused to ring. The urge to call Summer was powerful, but the thought of possibly blowing her cover or interrupting whatever she might be doing to save Henry stopped me. I reached for the door handle and opened it slowly, the sound of sirens was faint now, and it may have been wishful thinking, but it seemed like there was smoke rising up from somewhere in the vicinity of the compound. I was about to climb down from the cab when cars began trickling away from Pastern and onto the highway. It was enough to give me pause.

Indecision held me frozen. *Just do something already.* The internal pep talk moved on to pleading for another plan to form, or a sign for what to do next. When neither came, I went to slam the driver's door shut if only to dispel some of my exasperation. But before I could, a hand reached up and grabbed to door's frame.

I couldn't contain my scream, it bounced around the cab and escaped back out the now wide-open door. I thrashed, continuing to scream, and tried to scramble back farther into the truck as two large hands reached in to grab me.

'Kaly, it's me. You need to be quiet!"

It took a moment for his words to reach me, and then another moment for me to stop pushing him away and instead pull him into a brief hug.

"Gaël," I said breathlessly. "You're okay. Right? You're okay?"

He nodded.

"Where's Henry? Is he all right?"

"We split up, we were going to meet back up out here by the road and regroup."

"I haven't seen him." My tone was frantic, and I made no effort to steady it. "We have to go back in and get him!"

He placed a gentle hand on my arm. "Let's give him a few more minutes. He's resourceful; I'm sure he'll be here soon."

The squeal of tires and quiet whine of an electric engine suddenly drew our attention. A flash of red streaked out from Pastern's private entrance and skidded sideways onto the highway.

"It's Summer!" I cried, when my brain finally caught up to what I was seeing.

"She's got Henry with her!" Gaël added.

I drew in a deep breath and relief flooded through me, but it only lasted a moment. Two black SUVs with tinted windows and oversized tires flew by us, in pursuit of Summer and Henry.

"Get in!" I practically yanked Gaël across my lap.

He awkwardly climbed toward the passenger side, mumbling apologies as he stepped on my toes and kneeled on my fingers in his scramble over me.

I cranked the keys in the ignition and the engine roared to life. I cringed as heavy tree branches scraped the sides of the truck, like nails on a chalkboard. We nearly ran a green pickup off the road as I swung our lumbering vehicle around to join the chase.

"What's the plan?" Gaël asked, tightly gripping the handle over the passenger door.

"We have to help them." I glanced at him briefly but then locked my eyes on the road, looking for any sign of the SUVs or Summer's cherry-red coupe. When I couldn't see either, I clamped down harder on the gas pedal.

Gaël's gaze was so heavy I could feel it. "We need a plan."

"Unless you have something more useful to say, I'm going to need you to shut up." I immediately regretted saying the words.

I swerved into the passing lane to get around a slow-moving minivan, hoping the jarring motion of the truck was enough to distract from my harsh words.

"I think we should get to the rendezvous point." His kind voice drove daggers of guilt through me.

I finally, briefly, let my eyes flick over to him, not bothering to hide my panic. "We can't just leave them! Pastern's goons are in those SUVs; we have to help them."

"Summer can lose them. She knows this area and her car is fast. We, on the other hand, are in a cumbersome, conspicuous truck and don't know this place at all. We will make things worse if we keep on in our pursuit." His calm reassurance was almost enough to break through my adrenalin-filled need to fight.

Almost.

"There has to be something we can do." My voice sounded hollow and unconvincing, even to me.

Gaël reached a hand over to push my leg off the accelerator. My mouth dropped open at his boldness, and the shock of it was enough to keep from fighting against him now.

"Kaly, we have to get to the warehouse and trust Summer

to get Henry there safely."

I eased back into the slow lane and let our speed continue to drop. "But what if she can't?"

"If worse comes to worse and Pastern catches them…." Gaël moved back to his side of the cab.

Groaning, I almost stepped on the gas again.

"He's gotten himself out of worse situations," Gaël added quickly. "He can get himself out of this one, too. But we need to be where we said we'd be. He'll be counting on that."

It was this last argument that finally made me concede to his plan.

"Fine," I forced out through clenched teeth. "How do we get back to the warehouse?"

Gaël punched some buttons into the laundry truck's dashboard GPS.

"Take a right in one thousand feet," the woman's voice spoke through the cab's speakers.

The two of us were silent the rest of the way back, content to let the GPS lady do the talking. I searched the parking lot as soon as we rounded the warehouse. My heart sank at the wide-open, empty space. There was no sign of Summer's car anywhere. I turned the laundry truck around and parked so we weren't visible from the street but so we could see anyone entering the lot.

"They aren't here." I couldn't help but state the obvious.

"They'll come."

"But—"

He held up a hand. "They have to lose their tail first. That takes time."

I was about to protest, but he hopped out of the truck before I could. I followed his lead and got out as well. I watched him jog over to a set of rusted dumpsters and lift the lid. I knew what he was after but had no intention of helping him by getting near the foul-smelling receptacles. I crinkled my nose as he threw open the top of the middle container, I could imagine the putrid smell and took an involuntary step back. He hoisted himself up so he could reach down inside and soon returned with two large rolls of vinyl.

"Thanks for the help," he quipped, a smile tugging at his lips.

I made a face. "I knew you could handle it."

He chuckled. "Well, I will definitely need help getting these new stickers on."

"Do you think this will be enough?" I asked as I helped him unroll the large image of a logo for a fictitious package delivery company.

"Enough to get us out of town." He peeled some of the backing off, and I helped him slowly smooth the new sticker on over the laundromat logo. "It's okay if they find the truck eventually. But we need to be long gone by then."

We were almost done when the burner rang inside my pocket. Gaël and I both looked at each other, hands frozen with the second sticker partially hanging from the side of the truck.

"I'm really starting to hate this phone," I muttered, pulling it free from my pocket and flipping it open.

Gaël finished up with the second sticker while I climbed back into the cab.

"Kaly."

His voice was like a cold compress on a fevered brow. Relief swept through me, and I gripped the phone tighter.

"Henry, where are you? Are you okay?"

I switched it to speaker phone, as Gaël climbed into the truck.

"We're still being followed." Henry's voice was tight. "Ditch the phone. We can't meet where we originally planned. Go to the fallback plan."

"I… fallback plan? What? Henry I don't understand. You can't get to the—"

Gaël grabbed the phone out of my hand. "We copy, good luck."

He folded the phone closed and lowered his window.

I nearly jumped out after it when he tossed it.

"What are you doing?!"

"Summer said the phones weren't secure, remember?" Like that was all the explanation needed.

"So?" I stared, as the only means of communication I had with Henry sat forlornly on the asphalt. It was nearly hidden by a line of large weeds that had pushed their way up through a crack in the pavement.

"It's not safe to talk on them, and we can't hold onto them anymore or they could track us. He was also telling us they can't get back here without announcing where *here* is. And finally, he was saying to head to a new meet up spot and they'll try to get there, too." His patient, composed voice was starting to get on my nerves.

"Try?" I was shouting and couldn't help it.

He held my gaze and took a deep breath, then another. On the third breath, I found myself mimicking him. That sneaky, little genius knew what he was doing, too, because on my second deep inhale he started to smile.

"Better?" He grinned.

"No," I pouted.

He grew serious again. "Henry's a big boy; he knows what he's doing, and he's faced worse situations."

My stomach churned at such a thought.

"We need to trust that he can handle himself and we need to do what he expects of us. Otherwise he will be too distracted worrying about us, and *that's* what will get him in trouble. Do you understand?"

"I know you're *handling* me." I brushed a few strands of my thick hair out of my face and glanced once more at the phone. "And I hate how good you are at it."

His expression softened. "I know what you care about, and I'm simply doing my best to address your concerns. When we're emotional, it can complicate things. The more clear-minded we can be right now, the better."

"Yeah, yeah, I get it, Mr. Spock."

He grinned at me and made the Vulcan salute with his left hand.

I bit back a chuckle as he leaned forward to punch our new destination into the GPS.

"Travel time is one hour and forty-five minutes." The feminine voice rang out in the stiflingly hot cab.

Once we were back on the road, I lowered my window. The cool, salty air rushed in as we picked up speed. "You know if you're wrong about what he meant by fallback plan, we won't know it for almost two hours."

Gaël shrugged. "It was the closest airport to us that's near the coast. That's where they're headed, I'm sure of it. Summer's exit strategy is sound. Pastern will be searching for the truck, so our long drive will make it even harder to track. And if they find it at the airport, they'll be looking at flights out and end up heading in the wrong direction."

"What if they suspect it's a diversion?"

"That's why we're making it so hard to find the truck. If they have to work to solve that mystery, they'll be less likely to suspect the misdirection."

We listened to the news station for as long as the signal carried it. The reports told us that firefighters were still battling the blaze at the Pastern compound. However Summer had managed to start the fire, she did it exceptionally well. They were predicting half the compound was engulfed already.

Gaël grunted when the radio signal finally succumbed to the static. "I can't wait to get back to the boat. I feel like I'm missing a limb without my tablet." He flipped the dial trying to find a new station.

"You're the one who said we couldn't bring any of that stuff with us," I reminded him.

"We couldn't take the chance that they could detect our tech." He rolled the dial past a classical station, a country station, and a station blaring lively salsa music; settling finally for a station playing songs from the '80s. When I didn't object, he leaned back in his seat. "I'm pretty sure that's what alerted them that first time. Summer said their detection equipment and software are highly advanced, though it's usually to make sure none of their projects get out as opposed to other tech getting in."

"Well, you should be back with your beloved tablet soon," I teased.

I was surprised at how easily the conversation came the rest of the trip. Gaël was normally so shy, I expected him to be less adept at holding such in-depth talks. But as long as it was a topic that interested him, he had no problem going on at length. And I was pleased to discover that my best friend was a topic that interested him. I happily answered his questions about her, and asked him things I knew she would want to know and probably would be too self-conscious to ask.

The nearly two hours went by much faster than I thought they would, and soon the GPS lady was telling us: "Your destination is ahead, half a mile, on your right."

I was about to step on the gas when Gaël murmured my name and kept his hand low to point to the side of the road. A police car waited patiently to catch wayward speeders. I hissed through my teeth but kept my speed steady, right at the posted limit. The last half mile seemed to take longer than the rest of the trip combined. But then we were turning into the short-term parking lot of the airport, and my frantic search made me forget everything else.

"They might not be here yet," Gaël warned.

"Her car is faster," I argued, searching the lot closest to the terminals for any sign of them. "They have to be here."

Not seeing them, we drove around to the long-term

parking lot. There were barely any cars this far back. Gaël started to say something as we pulled around a hedge of dark-green bushes, but I didn't hear him over my loud gasp.

I didn't wait for him to say anything else, I jumped out of the truck.

Chapter 17

I was in such a hurry to get out, I forgot to put the truck in park. But the sight of the car sitting in the nearly empty lot, glistening like a delicious, red apple, flushed all common sense from my brain. Only Gaël's quick thinking and even quicker reflexes kept the truck from rolling into a light pole.

Henry spotted us and started jogging in our direction. I hopped down from the cab and ran toward him, barely feeling my feet touch the ground.

It happened in slow motion, the foot hitting a patch of loose gravel, the hands reaching forward to catch the fall, the injured grimace, and the dreadful scraping noise followed by the sucking in of an aching breath.

"Not again," he uttered my catchphrase from behind his clenched teeth.

This time it was Henry on the ground, and the absurdity of the situation hit me hard. The relief and the laughter rushed through me in insuppressible waves. I collapsed in a heap next to him—half sobbing, half giggling uncontrollably and wrapped my arms around his neck.

"Are you all right?" Gaël came up next to us, concern

drawing his bushy eyebrows together.

"So much more than all right," Henry mumbled into my shoulder.

"Maybe you all can pull yourselves together long enough to get going? We still have to get to the boat," Summer called from over near her car.

"Right," I hiccuped and then attempted to pull myself together.

Henry pushed himself back to his feet and stood up, carefully brushing away the dirt from his cargo pants. He had since shed his light-colored laundromat coveralls for the more stealthy dark-colored clothes.

"Are you okay?" I asked as he helped pull me up.

"I was so glad to see you made it back safely," he brushed dust off his pants, "that I missed a step."

Gaël coughed, and when we looked over at him he was smirking at me. "We were talking earlier about how we can get distracted if we don't remain calm, weren't we?"

"What?" Henry's eyes bounced back and forth between us.

"Ignore him." I tugged Henry toward Summer. "Or he'll get more insufferable than he already is. If that's possible."

The bark of Gaël's laughter made me smile as we completed the trek to meet Ross at the boat.

"This wasn't part of the plan," Ross muttered to Henry, as we climbed aboard the boat with Summer in tow.

"We had to change the plan." Henry shrugged.

"We can't bring her with us yet," Ross wrung his hands.

"She hasn't been approved. You can't keep bringing whomever you want to the island, Henry. There are rules."

"*You're* the one who told her about us," Henry snapped. "*You* got her involved in this failed rescue attempt."

"It wasn't a total failure," I couldn't help but add. "We did manage to save these guys." I waved my hand over the crates strapped down in the boat.

"We came here for the Frission!"

Some of the primates stirred at Henry's shout.

I sucked in a breath.

"I'm sorry." Henry sighed and ran a hand through his hair, mussing it up until it was sticking up in most places. "But that was probably our only chance to get them back, and we blew it."

"We'll come up with another plan." I reached out slowly to touch his arm.

He placed his hand gently over mine. "Pastern now knows that *we* know where they are. They'll make sure to move them. I doubt we'll get lucky a second time."

There was a long silence.

Then Summer placed her hands on her hips and stared Henry down. "If you have half the brains in your little scientist commune that Ross claims you do, then it's only a matter of time before you outsmart Pastern. Ross says you're the best of the best. Why do you think I want to join you so badly?"

Ross cleared his throat and gave Henry a meaningful look.

But Summer seemed to understand what it meant. She

continued, "I just burned my career to the ground, literally. And I did it to save *your* bacon. You're taking me to your oh-so-secret base and your snobby group of mad scientists will vote me in because I'm also the best at what I do. And they'll be smart enough to want me on their team. Now let's stop lolly-gagging and get out of here before Pastern's creeps find us."

Gaël was the first to move, his quick, nimble steps taking him to the front of the boat, where he loosened one of the ropes that held us tight against the dock. Henry followed his lead and undid the rope at the back of the boat, and we were suddenly floating free on the gentle waves of the small bay. Ross shook his head but didn't say anything else as he took up a position at the helm. The motor grumbled slowly to life, and we were on our way.

"They're starting to wake up," Summer shouted to me over the noise of the engine and the rush of the water under us.

"We should get the drop clothes tied down over them if we can," I called back. "It won't keep them completely calm, but it should help some."

"Can't you dose them again?" Ross yelled from his post.

"I've already done it twice; I don't want to risk doing it again. Especially not out here."

As if to prove my point, the boat hit a wave and soared up into the air, only to fall back down in a bone-jarring splash.

Summer, Gaël, and I worked to cover the crates as best we could as a storm moved in along our trajectory. Henry tracked it on the sonar and tried to help Ross navigate the best possible route. A few animals began to chatter as thunder rumbled above us. Ross was finally able to hail Tunui on the radio and coordinated a plan to meet up.

It took us half an hour to reach Tunui and by that time we were all soaked and shivering. Our small boat had a few inches of water in the bottom and the drop clothes weren't doing much to keep our rescue victims dry. Summer and I did our best to console a whole lot of angry, scared primates. But the cracks of thunder and the roiling waves thwarted our efforts.

"Be careful moving those crates," Summer warned. "They're all riled up, it will make it even harder to carry them."

It was so incredibly worse than her warning. Between the storm rocking the boats, making the decks even more slick, and the agitated animals throwing themselves around their crates, it was nearly impossible to get them transferred.

The storm was so loud, I didn't even hear the splash. It was Summer's shrieking that made me stop what I was doing and rush to the side of our smaller boat in time to see Ross dive into the water.

"What's he doing?" Henry bellowed from up above on the deck of Tunui's boat.

"One of the crates fell!" Summer was pushing against the large boat, keeping the gap open between our two vessels.

I reached out to help her, searching the surface for any sign of Ross.

"He's going to get himself killed!" Henry quickly

climbed down and jumped over to where we were. He was starting to take off his jacket when Ross broke the surface, gasping and pushing a giant ball of fur up toward us.

The panicked creature seemed to come alive upon breaking the surface, it shoved Ross under in its attempt to get to safety. Summer reached for the soaked animal, and I helped her pull it from the cold sea.

"Keep the gap!" Henry called to me.

I looked and saw the boats starting to move together. I quickly reached out again and pushed with all my might, trying to hold our smaller boat away from the larger one. My arms shook from the effort, and I silently begged Henry to hurry.

Henry laid across the side of our boat and plunged his two large hands into the dark waters where Ross had last surfaced. A moment of struggle and then he was hauling Ross up and over the side and onto the deck. It wasn't a moment too soon, my arms gave way and the two boats crunched together as Ross lay dripping and panting on the deck next to me.

"Let's not drop any more monkeys, okay?" Henry patted Ross' shoulder roughly.

Ross was still laying prone on the deck. He laughed in between coughing fits. "Deal," he wheezed.

It took another hour to get the rest of primates transferred. Everyone moved slower and even more cautiously after Ross' little dip in the ocean. When we finally finished, Tunui cut the ropes and let the smaller boat drift away before starting the powerful engines and steering us toward the island.

We left Ross in one of the cabins, bundled up with several blankets. His new best friend was glued to his side.

The primate he rescued now clung to him, snuggling next to him under the warm blankets.

The rest of the animals were in a small cargo hold. We gathered two space heaters we found and cranked them up to help warm the wet and weary souls who stared out at us from the crates.

"Do we have any towels?" I asked Henry. And then to Summer I said, "Do you think they'd let us dry them off?"

Henry went in search of towels.

Summer shrugged. "Maybe. Do you think it's necessary, since we've got these heaters in here?"

"I think it would help." I nodded, practically having to shout over the cacophony of noise from the restless beasts.

We moved slowly and spoke gently, doing our best to towel dry the ones who weren't too riled up. And moved the ones that were too upset, closer to the heaters. Then we went in search of dry clothes for ourselves.

In one of the cabins, I found a pair of cargo pants that had to be cinched with some rope to keep them from falling down. And an oversized, fuzzy sweater sitting in a drawer was nearly enough to make me cry. I threw my wet, ruined overalls into the trash, happy to be rid of them. I stood for a moment and let the delicious warmth of the dry clothes and heated cabin soak into my extremities. After one last, glorious moment, I re-entered the cooler air of the hallway and set off in search of the bridge. That was where I'd find Henry.

The bridge was a small, enclosed area at the highest point of the boat. Monitors glowed and beeped under windows that lined three sides of the room. I could see nothing but ocean all around us. The storm had finally passed, but night was quickly approaching, gobbling up waves as it pressed the sun lower into the horizon.

Tunui stood at the wheel, his eyes flicked to me as I entered and then straight ahead, set on the course that would take us home.

"I can't get a hold of Art." Gaël was standing off to one side with Henry.

Henry was staring down at one of the many monitors, he frowned at Gaël's words and then looked up at his friend. "You were able to before?"

"Before we went ashore." Gaël nodded. "I haven't been able to communicate with him since we got back, though." He waved a tablet at Henry as though to emphasize his point.

Henry's frown deepened. "Maybe the storm is causing interference?"

Gaël scratched his head. "It always seemed like once Art was in a system or device that he could operate with autonomy. So long as my tablet is working, he should be able to *continue* to communicate with me."

"Maybe something happened with the Frission." Henry's brows knitted in concern. "Pastern is doing who-knows-what to them right now. Maybe it triggered a failsafe that shuts Art down."

"Could be," Gaël admitted. "Without Art, it's going to be even harder to find them again."

Henry blew out a breath. "I know. I was thinking the same thing."

"We'll find them," I said.

Both men turned to look at me.

"Hey. You found something dry to wear?" Henry was still in his damp clothes from before.

I did a sheepish twirl, immediately regretting it as soon as I finished. The dazzling smile that filled his whole face somehow made me feel more and less mortified at the same time.

"So you're," my voice cracked. I coughed and then continued. "You're having trouble reaching Art?"

Thankfully, Gaël ignored the awkwardness and answered without missing a beat. "Yes, it's quite concerning. Whether he went radio silent by choice or by coercion."

"So, what do we do now?" I asked.

But both men remained silent, Gaël staring at his tablet and Henry gazing out the window. I let the quiet fill the enclosed room until I felt like I couldn't breathe. The frustration and hopelessness was stifling.

When I couldn't take it anymore, I spoke, "We just need to re-group. We'll get the primates and ourselves back to Nowhere Island, then gather all those brilliant minds and figure out our next steps."

Henry's shoulders remained slumped. "Yeah, that sounds good."

I could tell his mind was elsewhere, and he didn't believe what he'd said. Sticking around was no longer an option for me: I had to get out of there.

"I'll go see about making us all some comfort food. We all need to replenish after the last few hours." I didn't wait for a reply; I simply left the bridge. No one tried to stop me, which caused me more concern than everything else thus far. It was a bad sign, a truly bad sign indeed.

The rest of the trip back to the island was excruciatingly uneventful. Normally, after such a harrowing experience, dullness would be a welcome respite. But with the fate of our alien visitors still unknown, it only left time for torturous thinking about all the "what-ifs."

Abe was working on something on the dock when Tunui cut the motor and let our craft glide into its slip.

The scientist stopped what he was doing and faced us. "Any luck?"

Ross glared at Henry when he shook his head, then Ross spoke quickly, not giving Henry a chance to say anything. "We had *some* luck. We got the primates we were after."

Abe seemed to realize what that meant because he added, "But you didn't get the Frission back."

Henry climbed over the side of the boat onto the dock. "We need to gather everyone for an emergency meeting. Come up with a plan for what to do next."

"Yeah, that's okay," Ross snarked. "We'll get all the primates off the boat. You go on ahead."

It was almost as if I could see the words hit Henry in the back of the head as it snapped slightly forward, and he spun around. He looked ready to give a rather unpleasant response when his eyes caught mine and his expression softened.

"I'll send some others to help." He seemed apologetic. "Sorry, Kaly, I can't stay. I feel responsible for what's happened. I need to get them back."

"I understand." I waved him off. "You go find our missing aliens. If anyone can, it's you."

His shoulders dropped a little, and his smile came easy this time. He gave me a wink. "Come meet us when you're done?"

I nodded.

He motioned for Gaël to follow him, and they briskly left the dock.

I headed for the stairs that led down to the hold. Ross fell in behind me.

"I'll never understand what you see in that man."

I glanced back and him, and he made a face like he was about to be sick. I turned back around and didn't give him the satisfaction of a verbal reply.

The primates started chittering loudly when we entered the cramped storage cabin. I grabbed the closest crate and spoke softly to the scared creature as I carried it back toward the door.

"You want them all in the exam room?" He interrupted my baby talk; I could tell he was trying not to laugh.

I turned away so he wouldn't see my cheeks turn red. "Yeah, I need to check them out, and then we'll have to introduce them to their new environment slowly."

"Lucky's going to flip! She's been begging for friends ever since I taught her the sign for it." His steps were slower and heavier than before.

My curiosity forced me to peek back. He was carrying one of the crates that had two primates in it. They were a little agitated but seemed to enjoy being together.

"That will need to happen slowly, too." I had to turn to watch my step going back up the small staircase. Tunui had the boat tied down and was waiting on the dock to help us unload. I grunted as I hefted the cage up over the side and handed it off before climbing over after it.

"Thanks." I gave Tunui a quick smile and took back the crate, then headed for the exam room.

It felt like it took days to get them all unloaded. I made two trips before my body decided it had had enough. Ross, Becca, and a couple other scientists whose names I didn't know came and brought the rest of the crates to the exam room. I supervised but couldn't do much more than that; my muscles were screaming from all my earlier exertion, and my eyes were starting to burn. I hadn't slept or showered in more than twenty-four hours, and I was feeling and smelling the part.

"I need sleep, food, and a hot shower… and some sleep," I informed Becca when all the animals were safely off the boat.

She giggled. "Yes, you do," she said with the honesty only a best friend can give.

"I'm going to go do just that," I mumbled, doing one last scan of the room. "If Henry is looking for me, tell him my plan."

"Okay, get some rest." She patted me on the back and then sniffed me. "Maybe the shower first, yeah?"

I gave her a half-hearted shove and then made a beeline

for my room. After my zombie shower, I collapsed into bed in my robe. The towel was still wrapped around my hair as I fell into a deep, dark sleep. Awoken much too soon by obnoxiously loud pounding on my door.

"Kaly, wake up!" It was Gaël.

I rubbed my eyes and sat up slowly. My muscles were stiff and revolted against me, and I fell back onto my pillow. Only then did I realize my hair was still partially in the towel.

"Here, let me." I heard Becca shout just before she barged in my room.

I groaned and carefully raised an arm to pull the rest of my tangled hair free.

"Kaly, it's Art." Becca came over and pulled me from the bed.

Another large groan erupted from my lips, as muscles I didn't even know I had all protested at once.

"Five more minutes, Mom," I begged.

"Henry needs all hands on deck." Becca shoved me toward the door. "Now that Art is communicating again, we're going to come up with a plan to get the Frission back, and he wants everyone's input."

A sudden realization hit me as we crossed the threshold of my room. "Let me at least get dressed first!"

She slowly let go of my arm. "Fine, you have one minute. I mean it, I'm timing you!"

I raced back into my room and threw on the first things I could find, which was a pair of Minnie Mouse leggings and an oversized sweatshirt of Henry's that he let me borrow when I told him how comfy it looked.

Becca was pushing my door open just as I was pulling it from the other side, and with that much force the inevitable happened: my face and the door collided.

"Not again," both Becca and I said at the same time.

"Are you okay?" She didn't wait for my response; she grabbed my arm and pulled me out into the common room we shared. "You're fine, let's go."

My face was finally done smarting when we arrived at the conference room. It was crammed full of what looked like every scientist on the island. There was barely enough room for us to squeeze in, too.

"What's the word?" Gaël asked Abe, who was standing near the door.

Abe shrugged. "No one will shut up long enough for us to hear what Henry's saying.

"Let's get closer," I suggested and started shouldering my way forward.

We worked our way over to where Henry was holding court. And Abe was right: it was loud enough that we couldn't hear Henry's conversation. He had his arm raised and his wrist communicator was flashing, which meant someone was talking, but I couldn't hear what was being said until we were standing right next to him.

We made it just in time to hear Art say, "My hosts are gone, Henry."

Chapter 18

The room slowly went silent.

"What do you mean gone?"

"They took the shuttle back to their ship and have left the Milky Way."

"That can't be right," Jacob butted into the conversation. "If their ship was gone, someone would have told me. But no one told me about it, so it can't be gone." His nearly manic eyes searched the room.

No one would meet his gaze.

"Right?" His tone reached a frantic pitch.

There was a long moment of silence before a short man with a thin mustache and horn-rimmed glasses coughed and took a shuffle step forward.

"We lost contact with the ship." He shoved his frames up with two fingers, and his eyes darted furtively around as Jacob's breathing grew ragged. "We thought it was the typical interference—you know, solar flares," the man explained in a squeaky voice.

I thought Jacob's head might actually explode, like you see in those cartoons where the character's face gets all red and steam starts to pour out of their nose and mouth. Though it wasn't actually steam, it was really more of a fine mist of spit as Jacob's breath forced its way free from his clamped lips. And instead of hearing that cartoonish kettle noise, it was more like a barley repressed scream from somewhere deep in his throat.

"That's not helping, Jacob," Henry said. "Let's all just take a second to calm down."

I flinched as the livid man of science took a swing at the man I loved. And in that moment, I didn't entirely blame Jacob. You don't tell an angry person to calm down, that's *Deescalation 101*.

The wild punch missed its mark as Henry deftly dodged it.

At the same time, without thinking, I stepped in between the two men to try to help defuse the situation.

"Kaly don't!" Henry's warning was too late.

Jacob wheeled around for a second go and instead of landing a fist on Henry's gloriously chiseled jaw, Jacob ended up socking me right in the eye.

Absolute horror crossed his face in the last few seconds of sight I had before my vision went white. But sheer adrenaline and experience with blows to the head kept me focused on what was likely to happen next.

"Stop!" I shook my head to clear away the explosion of colors flashing across my eyes and noticed that my shout succeeded in stopping Henry from retaliating.

The shock of what he'd done drained away the last of Jacob's anger.

"I'm fine!" I resisted the urge to put a hand up to my throbbing eye socket, knowing the gesture would only make things worse. "Everyone take a deep breath and let's try to think and talk this through. They're gone, they left. But it was *their* choice. Maybe we should find out *why*," I reasoned.

Henry tipped my chin up and peered closely at my quickly swelling eye. I batted his hand away and turned so he couldn't watch the bruise that was surely forming.

Henry sighed, lowered his hand to my shoulder, and gave it a quick squeeze. "Why did they leave?" He asked, turning his attention back to his wrist communicator.

"After being taken by Pastern, my hosts tasked me with perusing the company's databases and research files, and then any news clippings pertaining to them. They were more distressed by what I found there than they were in their own… to use your colloquialism, kidnapping."

"We told you Pastern was not to be trusted," Henry stated. "Wait, they had *you* do it? Which means you could communicate with them? Did you know where they were the whole time?"

"You seem to forget they are far more advanced than you," Art stated plainly. "They were never in real danger from Pastern. They simply wanted to collect more data on them. Pastern has closed servers, so getting inside their compound afforded my creators the opportunity to take a look at their data."

"And you didn't think to tell any of *us* this useful piece of information?" Jacob's voice was wobbling dangerously close to the edge of exploding again.

"My hosts gave me a direct order not to. They wished to see your reaction to the situation."

"We were being tested," Henry muttered, shoving his hands into his pockets. "And I suppose we failed at that, too."

"Apologies, Henry, though your concern and rescue attempt was admirable, my hosts still feel as though your species has not evolved enough to pursue a continued relationship at this time. Thus their decision to leave."

"You can't judge our whole species on that one group of people," I argued.

"It was not only about Pastern, Kaly," Art's southern twang sounded almost sad. "It was an aggregate of all the information I have collected since my arrival. They wish to wait until you have advanced more in your responsible and positive treatment of one another and your resources before they are willing to engage with you further."

A thought suddenly came to me, "Wait, but they left you behind?"

"I am a mere shell of my former programming," Art informed us. "They have modified my code so I might continue to monitor your progress, but I can do little else. They forced me to go quiet as they made their exit and only then allowed me to tell you all this once they were safely out of the solar system. I can no longer access schematics for their advanced technology, nor their superior, collective knowledge. However, I retain my ability to communicate with you, and I retain the knowledge of your species and planet that I have obtained since my arrival."

"Super," Jacob's voice was slathered in sarcasm.

"This encompasses all I have learned about tone and inflection," Art added. "Which includes detecting sarcasm, Jacob."

"Well great. We can't cure cancer, but if we need help detecting sarcasm, Art can help us." Jacob sneered.

The murmuring in the room grew louder.

"That's enough," Henry said just loud enough for Jacob to hear.

The other scientists began to argue, and the noise level continued to rise.

"No," Jacob snapped, nearly shouting to be heard over the din. "You know what's not helpful is this AI demoted to a Cracker Jack prize for—"

"That's enough," Henry ordered, and the room fell silent.

"So," Becca finally joined the discussion, "what do we do now?"

Henry took a deep breath and let it out slowly, but it was Gaël who spoke. "We do what they require. Make our world worthy of a second chance."

All eyes turned toward Gaël. I expected him to shy away from the attention, but it seemed to make him bolder.

He continued, "Our purpose for Nowhere Island hasn't changed. We came here to make a difference, to make the world better. We keep pressing toward that goal. Now, we have a little extra motivation to do it."

His smile was infectious. Many of the other scientists were starting to nod and grin back.

"And in the mean time, maybe we can speed up our space exploration a bit, too," Henry suggested with a twinkle in his eye.

A woman I didn't recognize pushed her way through the crowd and came up to tap Henry on the shoulder. He spun around, his eyebrows scrunching when he saw who it was.

"What is it, Shelly?"

"I know this isn't a great time, but I've got our lawyers from three different countries calling, and they're all losing their minds."

The sparkle in his eyes went dull. "The secrets out." I made a face at him that he seemed to read well because he explained, "The lawyers would only call for high-level issues, which means that the world knows about our visit and apparently several governments have linked that shuttle to us…. Well, to me and one of my corporations."

"The whole world knows?" I marveled. Living in our bubble here on the island made me forget that life was still going on elsewhere. And that people would most likely be freaking out when they learned we weren't alone in the universe. Only then did it dawn on me to ask, "Wait, how do they know, though?"

Henry placed a hand on my arm, and my heart picked up speed.

"Remember, I told you other radars would pick up their ship eventually. And once they knew it was there, it would be easy to track the movements of our shuttle. It was bound to lead back to us… er, me, eventually." He turned to Shelly. "I'll call them back and have them issue a statement."

The petite scientist shook her head, and her dishwater-blonde hair swung back and forth. "I don't think that will be enough." She rubbed her hands on her bright-pink slacks that matched her lipstick. "It's been all over the news. People are panicking. There are riots and protests. Countries are saber rattling over what will be done about the extraterrestrials. It might not be sufficient to make a statement. The lawyers are throwing around words like governmental black sites and congressional hearings."

"Riots? Protests?" I squeaked.

Her wide eyes bounced back and forth between me and Henry. "Yes, I suppose our species has never really been adept at handling such world-changing circumstances."

Henry ran a hand through his thick, dark hair. "Still failing their tests," he muttered.

I rubbed his back slowly, in a large circle. "You've got a whole island full of the smartest people. If anyone can figure out how to solve the world's problems it's all of you."

"Well, it has to be us, because we certainly aren't getting any help from the *superior* beings." Jacob made air quotes with his fingers. "Or their pet robot."

I felt the inexplicable need to defend Art. "That's not helpful."

Henry turned to address the whole room. "To say this news is disappointing would be devastatingly inadequate. And I know it feels like it's created far more problems that seem to outweigh the thrill of our encounter. But we cannot forget that we discovered life! It exists elsewhere in our universe. This opens up so many doors for future discovery and innovation. If this doesn't fire you up to get back to your labs and carry on, I don't think anything will."

Jacob opened his mouth to say something, but Henry continued before he could. "And denigrating the AI that actually allowed us to *meet* extraterrestrials in the first place is unnecessary and unfair. Prior to these recent events, Art has been extremely helpful. And we must remember he is a program and must do what his authors instructed him to do. Even if that means his assistance is now limited."

"You will find that even in my current state, not all of my help is trivial," Art cut in. "For example, I can now tell you with ninety-eight percent certainty who your file thief is. Though they have already fled the island."

The room erupted into tumultuous shouting again.

"Who's missing?"

"Someone left the island. Did anyone know that?"

"How did we not know any of this?"

"This has all gotten completely out of control!"

"Why is this robot the only one who knows what's going on around here!"

The questions tumbled out as everyone in the room spoke over one another.

"Quiet!" Henry finally bellowed. It took the room longer to settle this time, but once it did he continued in a softer voice. "Who is it, Art? Who's been stealing our files, and did they take anything else before they managed to get away unnoticed?"

"It is Kalypso."

"How do you know it's her?" Someone asked from

somewhere near the back of the room.

Jacob nodded his approval of the question. "Yes, and how do you know she's even gone?"

Everyone started looking around, as though Lips might suddenly appear and prove the AI wrong.

Art spoke up. "I have accounted for everyone else through their communicators and specific biometrics that are recorded through said devices."

My cheeks grew warm. I had no idea my wristband could do that and for some reason it left me feeling like my privacy had been violated.

"Her communicator is recording metrics that do not match her specific signature."

"You can tell who someone is just from that?" My voice was hoarse, and I had to clear my throat halfway through my question.

"Yes," Art stated plainly. "This indicates she removed the band and attached it to some other living organism. When I noticed this anomaly, I did a quick survey of the island's scanners and found that there are no mammals large enough to be human that do not have a communication device. At least none that don't also have a tracking tag that all the animals have. This means she is no longer on the island. I then did a search of the GPS of every mode of transportation that could potentially leave the island and found that one was deactivated. A search of all of the security cameras revealed that one of the emergency crafts is missing." The AI's southern twang was suddenly a little less charming.

"So we know she's not on the island," Henry repeated

slowly. "Art, is there any way to tell *when* she left?"

"It was at some point while I was in my, what you might call a 'time out.' She sprung Gaël's trap right before my creators placed me on lockdown, or I would have informed you sooner. This leads my reasoning program to deduce that she took all the missing files and fled the island."

"A trap? Gaël set a trap? Why are we only now hearing about this?" Jacob hollered.

Gaël ignored Jacob's question and instead asked one of his own. "Henry, if Lips left the island, the bigger concern is if she discloses our location. What's to stop her from selling this information to any interested parties?"

"Nothing." Henry shook his head.

"So what do we do?" I asked, though I was absolutely sure I wouldn't like the answer.

"We have no choice." Henry scrubbed his hand over his face. "We have to evacuate the island."

The room erupted into chaos again.

Henry held his hands up, making a motion that requested quiet.

When the group complied, he continued. "I know it won't be easy, but we do have the framework in place to get a new lab set up as quickly as possible." People began to murmur, so he raised his voice. "Though we took extensive measures to make sure *this* wouldn't happen, we always knew it was still a possibility and wanted to be ready for it. Now that it *has* happened, we won't panic. We will evacuate immediately and begin the process of putting a new lab together.

"In the mean time, we have a freighter we can utilize to store equipment, data, and all high security and sensitive research projects. The freighter can hold a skeleton crew, so any researchers who need to can stay with their projects to keep them stable and make sure no longterm or necessary ongoing data collection is lost. Anyone else will have to lay low until we get things up and running again. Then we'll send for you as soon as we're able."

"What about the animals?" I asked, thinking of how hard it would be to find such an ideal location for a new Sanctuary.

Something indiscernible flashed in Henry's eyes. "They'll have to stay here for the time being."

"Someone will have to stay to take care of them." Ross' tone didn't make it sound like he was volunteering.

Henry nodded.

"Won't that be dangerous?" Ross continued.

"Tunui and his wife have agreed to stay if this plan ever needed to be enacted," Henry explained. "And of course, I will be staying until we can move everything permanently to our new location. George and Gaël, I would like to task you with spearheading the search for our new spot."

The two men nodded a little too quickly for them to not have known about this contingency plan.

I didn't have time to think about it more, because Henry continued, "With everyone else and all our research off the island, it should lower the level of danger."

Should lower. I felt like the breath had been knocked out of me. The situation was dire, but someone had to stay to care for the animals, and no one was rushing forward to volunteer.

"I'll stay." The words were out of my mouth before my brain truly registered what I was even saying.

Henry looked at me for a moment. "Are you sure?"

My brain finally caught up and was screaming at me not to stay; the danger was still too great. But my heart was running the show and my mouth. Once more the words came out quickly, "I'm sure."

"What about the files she took?" Jacob interjected.

Like a flock of seagulls, we all turned our heads toward him like he was our next meal. He shrank back a bit.

"What files were they?" Henry's piercing gaze soon had Jacob fidgeting like mad.

"Um, well, I'm not sure what she took. I'd have to look and see what's missing," The shorter scientist mumbled.

"I can tell you," Art's voice rose up from Jacob's wrist communicator.

Jacob quickly clamped his hand over his wrist. When he noticed our suspicious looks, he let go and swung his hands behind his back. "Of course you can, because you are oh-so helpful. Why don't you put yourself to better use and find out where Lips went?"

Art's twang seemed thicker than ever. "Unfortunately, because of my new limitations, my days of carefree galavanting have been brought to an end. I am only able to exist within the systems of the island until you are able to upgrade me with knowledge learned here on Earth."

"Par for the course," Jacob muttered.

"What files are missing, *Art*?" Henry asked more forcefully this time.

Jacob wouldn't look anyone in the eye as Art answered.

"They are schematics for a device that scans and interprets brainwaves."

My mouth fell open.

"Does it work?" Henry's voice was half awestruck, half concerned.

I was finally able to break free from my dumbstruck moment. "You can read people's minds?!"

"Such a rudimentary description." Jacob's tone suggested displeasure, but he was nodding his head enthusiastically.

Henry took a step closer to the other scientist. "Does. It. Work?"

Jacob was suddenly fascinated with an invisible speck on the floor. "I'm not sure," he responded. "I didn't have the chance to build a prototype yet. But earlier designs lead me to believe that yes, it would work."

Chapter 19

"Think of the implications of this," Gaël spoke animatedly to Henry.

We were seated once more in the outdoor dining area halfway up the mountain, the same beautiful place where we ate our first night on the island. But the views weren't holding our attention tonight, the discussion was.

We had been there long enough for the sun to set and the stars to come out. Though they went largely unnoticed. The time passed in deep talks about our disappointment in the way things had ended with the Frission and wound around to the topic of Lips absconding with Jacob's research and the science behind his nascent invention.

"We're still not sure if she took anything else with her when she left." Henry rubbed his temples. "And I can't even begin to think what she'd want with Abe's jellyfish research. I don't see any connection."

"The immortality of jellyfish and mind-reading capabilities—what more could a future evil dictator want?" I quipped.

Gaël frowned at me. "Lips never struck me as wanting to do anything potentially harmful to others."

"You obviously never paid attention when she looked at me," I muttered.

"I can't help but think of all the good that can come from Jacob's invention," Gaël continued, oblivious to what I said. "People who are nonverbal will be able to communicate!" He was practically effervescent. "There are so many exciting, potential applications for such a device."

"Do you know how dangerous it could be? What an invasion of ultimate privacy it is?" I countered, finally feeling justified in my animosity toward Lips. "Especially if it falls into the wrong hands, which is exactly what seems to have happened. It would be like *1984* on steroids."

"I have the best investigators money can buy out looking for her," Henry added weakly.

"What will you do when you find her?" I stared him down.

He wouldn't meet my gaze. "Get back whatever she took."

"And then?"

A heavy sigh was his only response.

The four of us grew quiet as we all gazed down at our plates of uneaten food.

"This day needs to be over." Becca spun some grilled asparagus around on her plate. "Just when I think it can't get any worse, it does."

"Becca's right," Henry announced.

My brows knit in confusion.

Henry tried to smile but couldn't manage more than to raise one side of his enticing mouth. "We should all go get some sleep. We've got a lot to do the next few days."

It was like the weight of everything hit us all at once. No one argued or had anything else to say. We all got up slowly and made our way to our rooms. Quiet 'good nights' were mumbled and doors clicked softly behind us as we turned in. I would have been surprised at how easily I fell into sleep, but it happened so fast, I didn't have time to think about it.

The evacuation was so efficient it made my head spin. It wasn't long before I found myself alone with Henry in our favorite picnic spot, only this time knowing that the island was entirely deserted. Even Tunui and his wife had gone on one last supply run, leaving us completely isolated. It truly made the place feel like Nowhere Island.

"Shouldn't we be doing something," I asked, feeling guilty for lounging while it felt like the rest of the world was falling apart. "There's still gotta be a lot to do to get things ready for the new location. Or world leaders to meet or angry mobs to calm. And we're just sitting here having a meal."

"I think we deserve a bit of a break. After everything we did to evacuate? And my lawyers are meeting with the heads of state so we don't need to get involved with that. And honestly, I don't think any angry mobs would listen to us even if we tried. So let's take some time to bask in the calm here for a bit."

Henry's grin was infectious, and I soon found myself beaming back at him like an idiot.

"I suppose a little break wouldn't hurt." I shrugged.

He looked at me thoughtfully. "But speaking of getting the *new* location ready...."

The way he said new made my curiosity spike. His following silence drove me to press the matter. "What about it?"

"There's something I've needed to tell you, but I wanted to wait until we were alone."

Goosebumps rose on my arms, and I realized I was holding my breath.

He looked at me in earnest. "It's a secret about the island that only a handful of people know."

I frowned—not where I thought he was going, but I was still intrigued. "Okay."

"Would you believe a whole island can move?"

Pausing, I let the words rattle around in my brain. "Honestly, I'm still not sure I believe in aliens and yet we saw some." I laughed. "So I guess I can't say a moving island would be that hard a pill to swallow, why?"

As soon as I finished saying the words, the realization of what he was implying hit me.

"Nowhere Island can *move*?" I felt stupid saying it, but I was at a loss for other words.

"I thought it was a volcano? How do you move a volcano?"

"Very carefully."

I couldn't help but scoff at his bad joke.

"They won't see it coming!" Henry announced triumphantly.

"So Gaël, Becca, and the rest of the exploratory committee are out there looking at potential new locations for no reason?"

He grew serious. "They are doing it to throw anyone who's watching off the trail."

"Do *they* know that?"

"Gaël knows; the rest of the group doesn't," Henry admitted. "And I'm not sure if Gaël told Becca or not. Those two have become close lately. But I don't know *how* close."

I was silent for a moment, trying to wrap my head around it all. Finally, I said, "That will make it easier on the animals I suppose. But you don't think your brainiac scientists will notice everything looks exactly the same and figure it out?"

"We'll change the labs, mess hall, and med bay up a bit," Henry explained. "Tunui is already working on some projects to modify things. The blueprints for this lab are pretty basic. Originally, we had to build most of it offsite and then bring it here. We'll tell everyone we went off the same schematics because it was faster than starting from scratch. The hardest part is detaching from the geothermal vents and finding a new place to essentially hook us up again."

"What about when people go outside?"

"My colleagues aren't really the outdoorsy types, most of them barely stepped foot outside the whole time they were here. And if they did, they stuck to the small recreation pavilion we built and the place where the animals are first brought when we reintroduce them to the outdoors. We've got a plan for completely changing the way those two places look."

I gave him a skeptical look.

He continued, "We built this island to look like a

number of other volcanic islands out there. In fact, those are the ones Gaël will take the exploratory committee to. It will help sell it to the others."

"Wait, you *built* this island?!"

Henry nodded slowly. "We wanted it to be moveable, so our options were to build it ourselves or try to dig out an already existing island. Building it was the simpler solution. Our very own Dr. Schotzberg had invented an oversized 3D printer for the construction of homes in third-world areas. So we used his schematics to build an even larger printer that was capable of building this island. Then we found our thermal vents and hooked up our volcano."

I couldn't think of anything better, so I asked, "What did you use for your printing material?"

His smile grew and his eyes sparkled. "Plastic, the island is made of plastic we collected from the ocean. You ever hear of the Great Pacific Garbage Patch?"

My lips twitched and turned up at the corners when I could no longer fight the smile. "So you made an actual island, out of the trash island?"

His chest puffed out and his smirk grew wider. "Yep."

Scooting closer, I reached out to tug on the front pocket of his shirt. "Has anyone ever told you, you're super cute when you let your nerdy side show?"

"Not as often as they should," he joked as he leaned in to kiss me slowly.

My lips tingled in the aftermath of his passion. He reclined fully with his hands behind his head. I lowered myself down until I was nestled with my head against his chest. We laid there silently, listening to the soundtrack of the tropical evening.

"It's hard not to feel like it's all been a waste," he finally spoke, his voice full of sorrow.

I leaned up onto my elbow so I could look him in the eye. I knew him well enough now to follow his sudden change of subject. "I get that. The whole climax of meeting aliens was kinda blown to pieces by their abrupt departure."

He stared up at the sky.

My heart hurt to see him so discouraged, so I wracked my brain for words to say to ease his pain. "But we can't forget that we met honest-to-goodness aliens. They exist; we're not alone in the universe. So they want us to get our act together before they stop by for another visit. But honestly, that's why you all came to this miracle island in the first place: to help the world get its act together."

"I've been thinking about that," he finally replied. "With all the riots and unrest going on around the world, I don't think we have the right people we need to fix *all* of the worlds problems."

I gave him a funny look and he continued, "Don't get me wrong, we've got a lot of the right people here to solve things like resource shortages, environmental problems, health issues, things like that. But we also need people who can solve other problems like dealing with greed, blind ambition, and cruelty."

"There are people out there that can solve those problems?" I said jokingly.

But his face remained serious. "There's gotta be. We just

have to find them and give them the resources they need to come up with the right solutions."

"Sounds like a good plan. Count me in." I leaned closer to his face, pleased to see his cheeks redden for a change.

"Nowhere Island 2.0. We'll get it right this time." He smiled up at me.

"If there are people out there who can solve the world's problems, *you'll* be the one to find them and get them on board."

He quickly brushed his lips against mine and tucked a stray strand of hair behind my ear. "You mean *we* will find them and convince them to help."

I nodded. "Yeah, you and me." My head spun with all the giddiness that felt like it was bubbling up from my chest. "We'll figure it all out together."

He jumped up from our blanket and held out his hand to me. I grabbed it and he pulled me to my feet.

Giving me his brilliant smile that made me fall more in love with him every time it made an appearance, he said, "Well then, grab your toothbrush and let's go save the world!"

THE END!

ABOUT THE AUTHOR

Kara Piazza is the author of the prequel *The Maladroit* that tells the origin story of Kaly's journey prior to *Nowhere Island*. She is also the author of a soon-to-be-released, exhilarating novel, *The Seeker Initiative*. *Seeker Initiative* is a full-length, young adult novel, and it will be the first book in the series she has planned for her protagonists. She also authors The Writing Piazza Blog, where she documents her journey through the harrowing process of writing and publishing. Kara currently lives in Arizona with her amazing twin boys, and their spunky, fun-loving dogs Chico and Mushu.

You can connect with Kara through her website www.thewritingpiazza.com/blog/ or through social media.

Facebook: www.facebook.com/thewritingpiazza
Twitter: @writingpiazza
Instagram: @thewritingpiazza